HANNE ØRSTAVIK

Ti Amo

Translated from the Norwegian
by Martin Aitken

archipelago books

Library of Congress Cataloging-in-Publication Data available upon request.

Archipelago Books
232 3rd Street #A111
Brooklyn, NY 11215
www.archipelagobooks.org

Distributed by Penguin Random House
www.penguinrandomhouse.com

Cover art by Edvard Munch
Book design: Gopa & Ted2, Inc

This work is made possible by the New York State Council on the Arts with the
support of the Office of the Governor and the New York State Legislature.

Funding for the publication of this book was provided by a grant from the Carl Lesnor
Family Foundation. This publication was made possible with support from Lannan
Foundation, the National Endowment for the Arts, the New York City Department of
Cultural Affairs, and NORLA (Norwegian Literature Abroad)

Printed in the United States

Ti Amo

I LOVE YOU. We say it to each other all the time. We say it instead of saying something else. What would that something else be? You: I'm dying. Us: Don't leave me. Me: I don't know what to do. Before: I don't know what I'll do without you. When you're not here anymore. Now: I don't know what to do with these days, all this time, in which death is the most obvious of all things. I love you. You say it at night when you wake up in pain, or between dreams, and reach out for me. I say it to you when my hand finds your skull, which has become small and round in my palm now that your hair is almost gone, or when I stroke you gently to get you to turn over and stop snoring. I love you. Once, I would reach out in the night to touch your skin, to place my hand on your back, your stomach, your thigh, anywhere at all, and there'd be connection, contact. And in that feeling of skin and warmth, something small and without language, something perhaps undeveloped in me, a newborn part, could sink down to sense the base of night, return home, or arrive. I love you. But you are no longer in your body, I don't know where you are. Awash in morphine, you drift in and out of sleep or languor, and we do not talk about death, I love you, you say to me instead, and reach out for me from the bed on which you lie through the days, fully dressed, writing on your phone, writing a novel on that little screen, two or three lines at a time before you drift into sleep again, and I let go of the door frame and step towards you and take your hand and look at you and say: I love you, too.

"Language difficulties"
The relationship to reality is what matters,

wrote Birgitta Trotzig in the mid-seventies when I was six or seven years old. I saw her one autumn at the book fair in Gothenburg, it must be ten years ago now, probably more; we were both on our way from the Stadsbiblioteket to the main site, she on the opposite sidewalk in a long black skirt, limping slightly, from hip troubles, perhaps. A year or two later, I read that she was dead.

When it comes to what really happens to me, in life, I'm struck into silence. Silence! Stop sign – zone border! It becomes almost physically impossible for me to as much as register facts, dates – at least periodically. The real-life event *hits me, massively burdensome and complicated, overwhelmingly intangible – and transforms all speech, any form of direct articulation, into an unreal rustling of leaves.*

When did it all start? When did you actually become ill? Were you already ill that January we were in Venice, nearly two years ago, and you vomited and pulled out of your business dinner and the talk you were supposed to give? Three days later, we went to India. Were your cells already then frenetically dividing as we sat in the darkness, in a rowboat on the river, and watched the funeral pyres on the ghats of Varanasi?

Were you already ill then, in January 2018? The next time was June. I'd been at the book festival in Aarhus and we met up in Copenhagen. We'd rented an Airbnb on Islands Brygge, with a pull-out couch and the tiniest of bathrooms, a second-floor flat with a little balcony from where we could see the mouth of the harbor, the canal on the right. We met up on Saturday. I came in on the train, you'd taken a flight and were already checked in when I got there, you'd picked up the key from the host, who'd told us to say we were friends of hers if anyone asked. She was a singer, and we made up stories in which we were Norwegian and Italian musicians, I a cellist, you a violinist. But we didn't see anyone. The next day, we went out early and just walked, through the city center, into the northern quarters beyond the city lakes, streets we'd never walked before, we veered left into Vesterbro, and then suddenly, as we got to Kødbyen, the old meat-packing district, you had to stop and hold onto the corner of a building. You couldn't walk another step. It was impossible to tell if you were exhausted or in pain, you were almost angry with yourself. We took a taxi back to the flat.

We ate outside on the balcony all three nights. You hadn't the strength to go out looking for somewhere. It was nice, we both thought so. In bed you sat up, bent double in the night, such was the pain in your back. I'm not sure how much you slept, if you could even sleep like that. I kept waking up and you'd be sitting there next to me, bent double. Only now I remember you weren't well before that either, two weeks before, at that wine festival in Bordeaux. You'd been there years ago with a friend and so much wanted to go back again, with me, to amble about with a wine glass in a holder around your neck, pausing at the various tasting stations, trying the different wines and rinsing your glass in the little fountain before moving on to the next. We went to Bordeaux before I was due at the book festival in Denmark. We'd booked a room at a little two-star hotel, there were windows on two sides, one facing out onto a park, French windows extending to the floor, and we didn't eat out in Bordeaux either, despite you being so fond of eating out, we stayed in the room with wine and cheese, bread and couscous salad from the supermarket. You hadn't the energy. And in the night you were in pain. You hardly mentioned it.

From my point of view, something happened during the spring of 2018. It was as if the flame began to dwindle. The energy went out of you, and I thought it was to do with us. That we'd gone into a slide and that living with you, my whole reason for uprooting to Milan, was now going to tail away, until there was nothing left but a bare minimum of energy, a minimum of intensity.

I was jealous of your pain, which mounted over the summer. You'd wander about at night in our dark, roomy apartment, moaning and whimpering. It never occurred to me that you could be seriously ill. I reasoned the pain was from keeping something inside, that you weren't happy with me anymore and didn't want the life we were living, only you couldn't bring yourself to acknowledge it and tell me. That was what I thought. Sometimes I wondered if there was someone else, and would convince myself of it, that some other woman had become the object of your desires. For you were giving so little away, the signals you sent me were so unclear.

When we went to Venice again that August, to stay in the apartment the publishing house leases in Giudecca, you were in such pain the first night that it frightened both of us. When morning came, I phoned my father in Oslo. He used to be a medical worker and told us we should go to the hospital and get it checked. It was what we needed to hear, and we left at once. I remember the terror we felt as we clung to each other on the vaporetto, how we jumped ashore at the Zattere and hurried over to the Accademia, crossing the long, arching bridge that spans the Grand Canal, scuttling through the streets, past the church of Santa Maria dei Miracoli to the Campo Santi Giovanni e Paolo and the Fondamente Nuove where the hospital lies, surely the most beautiful in the world. Weak with trepidation, we searched the corridors for the emergency room, the building consuming us. We passed through an atrium with plants and trees and cats, until at last we found the waiting room with its blue plastic chairs and take-a-number dispenser, and when you came out again after registering and we looked up at the electronic board, there was a red dot beside your number. Only a few were red, most were green or yellow, and it took only a moment to realize they were the ones who would have to wait the longest. We understood that red was for alarm and emergency.

They called you in and made me wait outside. What did I

do for all those hours? I remember the sharp divisions between light and shadow, the heat, and the lions on the walls, emerging out of their painted fields, an illusion of depth where in fact there is none, only flat, bare stone. I hung around in the shade outside the entrance, went inside, came back out again. The square where the hospital is situated was a place I knew well, I'd crossed it so many times over the years, in all seasons, ever since I first started staying at the publishing house's apartment in the nearby Castello district. I remembered all the times I'd passed by those lions, marveled at the illusion, but had never gone inside. And now suddenly that Venetian hospital had become so acutely relevant to me. It was where they were going to find out what was wrong with you. You, with whom I belong. You, who make the night and the darkness our own, in our big bed, a place where I can touch you, sense that you exist, and feel secure. You, who are home to me, my sky. I clutch my phone. How long can this take? Hours without a word. There was no coverage in there, you tell me later. I don't know what I did with myself in all those hours, they come over like shards of images that don't belong together, a cobblestone, a door frame, a cat crossing the lawn in the heat, and everything too close up.

Sometime late in the afternoon, it must be nearly five o'clock, you're able to text me and tell me you'll soon be done, that I can come and fetch you, the name of the department. I go back inside and probe the corridors, searching, asking directions, at last to be admitted into a waiting room for relatives. But you're not there. I sit down on a chair, then switch to another, and the people already waiting belong together in little clusters, I'm the only one on my own. Several of the patients are in wheelchairs, some hooked up to IV, mobile drip stands at their sides, sitting with people I assume are their families, and their wheelchairs make me afraid: Not yet, I think to myself. Not you. Is this what's next?

And then you appear, in a wheelchair. You're pale, but smiling. I told them I didn't want the chair, you say, but they told you they were brand new and had to be used. There's nothing wrong, you say, and I burst into tears, again. I'm right as rain, you say. The pain in your stomach has eased too, you say. The doctor said only you would know what was giving you such pain. In other words: it was psychosomatic, something emotional.

They checked your heart. The red dot was for your heart, and there's nothing wrong with your heart.

We're happy, and trembling with relief, and you have to wait a while in your wheelchair, something to do with the medication that needs to kick in before you go, but it doesn't matter, because you're fine and we're together. Afterwards, we go out into a glow of low Venetian sun, buoyant, our minds at rest, and I can't remember what we did, where we went, maybe to the hole-in-the-wall place by the Rialto fish market, they open at six and serve little bocconcini with baccalà or ham, and strong Campari spritzers in long-stemmed glasses. We find room to sit, but mostly people just stand around on the little square with their drinks, Venetians on their way home from work, who've picked the kids up from school or daycare and then come back out before dinner, the few who still actually live here, enjoying their normal Monday-apéritif lives, their standing-about-chatting, drink-in-hand lives, in which everything is normal and the alarm of death hasn't just now sounded inside them and rendered everything else so depthless and unreal. Is that where we land, trembling and elated, to sit in the aftermath, fears allayed, with a drink and an appetizer? I can't remember. I text my father to say it was nothing. He replies immediately, glad.

But they didn't check for cancer. It didn't occur to me at the time, and I'm not sure it occurred to you either. We only think about it later. And about what the doctor said: "Only you know what's happening in your life that could make you feel such pain in your stomach now."

Two weeks later, we're at a reception for a writer at the home of one of your colleagues, all sparkling wine, white sofas and modern art, hired waiters in uniform circulating through the rooms, refreshing people's glasses and offering snacks from their little black trays, I'm on the prosecco, but all you want is water, you're not feeling well, you say, and that's how it's become, you never really feel like doing the things we did before, the things we did for fun together, in Venice I noticed you'd have a spritzer with me at the waterside café in Giudecca as the sun went down, every night we'd do the same thing and I know you were only doing it for me, because you knew it was what I wanted, that I wanted everything to be all right again, and you wanted that too, you'd have a spritzer and a tramezzino or a cicchetto, but without really wanting to, not even after the hospital had said everything was fine, and we ate at home in the evenings there too, unlike before, when the evenings had been new and lay open in front of us, when you'd be the most eager of us to go out and explore the streets for places we'd never been. It wasn't like that anymore.

And I see you sitting on the edge of that white sofa with your glass of water, when suddenly you thrust it into my hand and jump to your feet, leaving me dumbfounded as you dash for the loo. And I get up and follow, and as I reach the door I can hear you being sick. And I go in to find you bent double over the toilet bowl, and it's as if a river is running out of you, not food, not the lunch you've eaten or something you just drank, no, what's spewing out of you is black, liters of it, or so it seems, like thick, viscous oil, and afterwards we realize it's blood.

Ti amo. You're lying on our bed in the light, it's January 5, 2020, 3:10 pm, and we stopped by the Turks on Viale Papiniano and had a kebab for lunch, you drank two cans of Coke, it's Sunday and the sun is shining. A week from tomorrow you're going in for a new MRI scan and then we'll see if the lump both of us can clearly feel now on the right side of your stomach is cancerous or just a cyst of scar tissue. Here, you say, can you feel it? It's probably from the operation, don't you think? It's right where they put the tube in, and you indicate the little red indentation in your flesh, the tube they put in to drain the blood and pus from the abdominal cavity, and whatever else came out of you that way in the days that followed, when you lay in a hospital bed in a bright-blue pajama top with a catheter in your nose and still looked the same as you used to, before, when all this had only started, your illness, when it was still new to us that you were sick, when we still couldn't grasp it because it felt so strange, so wrong and unreal. And now more than eighteen months have passed and still we could claim with some justi- fication that we can't grasp it, that it feels so strange, so wrong and unreal. But it's not new anymore. Now it's just the way it is. You're dying. You lie in the bedroom, typing your novel into your phone, halfway through it now, you say, a sci-fi crime novel, as you've explained, and you're so completely wrapped up in it that when we have breakfast together on the sofa, or if

I just stand close to you for a bit, or sit down on the edge of the bed, and you look up at me and I ask you where you've gone, what you're thinking about, you jab a finger towards your head or the phone, and it means the same thing, that you're away inside your novel.

I too write, am writing this, the words I'm typing now, at this moment, in the study facing the rear courtyard, from whose window I can see rooftops and the dome of San Lorenzo, and far away in the distance the snow-covered peaks this side of Switzerland. It's Sunday, January 5, 2020, 3:17 pm now, and I'm writing this and you're still here, alive, in bed, presumably sleeping now, let me check... yes, you're asleep, you've turned onto your side and have fallen asleep.

When it comes to what really happens to me, in life, I'm struck into silence. Silence! Stop sign – zone border! It becomes physically almost impossible for me to as much as register facts, dates – at least periodically. The real-life event *hits me, massively burdensome and complicated, overwhelmingly intangible – and transforms all speech, any form of direct articulation, into an unreal rustling of leaves.* But still I know I must write, says Birgitta Trotzig. *And yet, the whole time, I sense deepest down, as strongly as if it were the life force itself, the desire to survive, that somehow I must connect with that real-life event in words, reach out to it, engage with it, take warmth from it.*

When you became ill, I was still finishing my previous novel. When we got you home from the hospital after the operation, and we were still living in that big, gloomy apartment then, just a single living space without rooms, like a hangar almost, or the lower section of some large pyramid, you confined to bed in the sleeping area, your enormous wound dressed and bandaged, a white bandage running from your chest to below your abdomen, there was nowhere I could go to finish writing my novel about a young woman who arrives in Milan to pursue her drawing and live with her new Italian partner, a novel about being parentless and thinking you can't be loved, that no one would want you, an awareness that precedes language and which the young woman is able to approach only in the pictures she draws, a novel itself comprised of pictures, in which her wounded urge for love quietly heals, the way sprigs and shoots will grow and put out the softest foliage and extend into what before was open and desolate and empty.

So I'd drop my Mac into a bag along with a charger and walk the half hour it took to get to the library next to the little park on Viale Tibaldi. It has a reading room with four rows of white laminated tables and strip lighting on the ceiling and there were always lots of other people there, there are so many people in Italy, everywhere's always so teeming with people that whenever I go back to Oslo after being in Milan for any length of time, it always takes me a while to get used to there being so few people in the streets and everywhere, and the Tibaldi library is full of young people listening to music on their earphones and chattering ceaselessly as if they were all joined together, connected up with each other in body and thought, as if the notebooks in which they write, the words and passages they highlight with their yellow and pink markers, were part of a great communal script that in some subterranean kind of way they're all logged into at once, in a world where no one else exists. There I'd sit with my novel, and no one ever knew who I was, that I'm a Norwegian writer writing a novel that's going to be published in a different country, while they're absorbed in their college work, and no one smiles at me at that library, the librarians don't, everything's crummy and clapped out, they're underpaid, and I've got a terminally ill husband at home, but we still think then that the surgery went well, that they've removed what needed to be removed, that the big lump which had grown so monstrously in the three weeks from you being diagnosed to the day of the procedure, so much so that the surgeon said afterwards that if he'd known it was that big he might never have agreed to operate, and then you'd have been dead now – then, then when I was working at the library.

I finish writing that novel there, and it's always dark, dark when I go there, dark when I go home again, dark in the apartment when I get back. You're in pain. You're unsteady on your feet and nauseous, and it hurts for you just to move. I finish writing that novel because it's the only thing I can do. I can't do anything to help you. I can't do anything for myself either, apart from that, finish the novel. Because it's what I do. I write novels. It's my way of existing in the world, I make a space for myself, or the novel makes a space for me, we do it together, and that's where I can be, inside the novel.

It was nearly finished when you became ill. I felt I needed to see it through, and at first I thought it was going to be hard, that it was perhaps even wrong of me to carry on working on it in that situation, like a detached technician processing my own life. But something happened between the two of us after you became ill which meant that the novel could finally come together. After you became ill, it was as if you needed to show me, in a different way, that I meant something to you, that in fact I meant everything to you. You asked me to marry you. You wanted to cement our relationship in formal terms. As if getting married could protect us, create a bond that could stop you from dying. Is that what we felt? That marriage was a silky red ribbon that would tie us together and give us something to hold on to, so that if death did come to snatch you away, it wouldn't be able to, because you were tied to me?

Feeling that you really wanted me was essential to that novel. I love you. I love you more than anything. You've always told me so. But until we got married there was something you never managed, that was impossible for you to express clearly to me. Somehow it just wouldn't come out. Was never quite clear. You. What you wanted. It wasn't the getting married that was important, it was you showing me what you wanted, that at last I could see what that was and how much it meant to you, and that it was so very, very clear to me that you wanted, and had chosen, me.

The fact that I perceived that so clearly meant that Val, the young woman in that novel, could come to an understanding of herself in Milan. For Val, the light she saw in that other person's eyes was like a lamp, illuminating at last the dark, lapping waters of the fjord outside the room of her birth, welcoming her into the realm of the new and all things possible.

And now I'm sitting here writing this.

This isn't the book I'd seen coming after *Novel. Milan*. My novels nearly always start with a place. It's how they come to me. I see, and know, where the story's going to be set. The book I was going to write after *Novel. Milan* wasn't supposed to be set here, at home in our apartment, in this study, with a view of rooftops and the dome of San Lorenzo. It was supposed to be set on another continent, in a city I barely know. That book is waiting for me there. But I've known all along that it can't be written until this is over. First, I had to know where we stood with your illness, what was going to happen. That you were going to get well again. The first couple of months after the operation, that still seemed like a possibility. But then, when the first MRI scan revealed liver metasteses, microscopic, but still, and I understood that you were going to die, I knew that I couldn't begin that novel until afterwards.

Why can't it be written before this is over? Because I know that writing it will involve exploring issues that I won't encounter until after you've gone. That I'll need to feel my way in and sense the nature of those issues as I go along. Only then will I know what the novel is about. So I can't do it yet. I don't know what I feel. I don't know what I'm going to feel. What questions will I have? I don't know.

Today is Monday, January 6. Epiphany. A bank holiday in Italy. A week from today you're going in for more tests. We have lunch on the sofa, florets of boiled cauliflower drizzled with olive oil, seasoned with salt and pepper, a wedge of gorgonzola and a salad you've taught me how to make: puntarelle chicory, sliced lengthwise, with a dressing made of the kind of anchovies we don't have in Norway, salty anchovies, very firm in the flesh, finely chopped and mixed with garlic and olive oil. I warm some bread to go with it. I unfold the low, rose-colored table in front of the sofa and put the food out on it, an IKEA version of the kind of tables we sat and ate street food at when we were in Vietnam, nearly three years ago now, the first faraway trip we took together, me having always wanted to go to Saigon, where Marguerite Duras went to school, and see the Mekong Delta, the landscape in which she grew up, and when I told you, right at the beginning, not long after we met, you said it would be our first winter trip, we'd go to Vietnam. And that was what we did. We spent ten days there, biking behind a guide, a skinny young Vietnamese guy, following the narrow pathways that criss-cross the network of rivers and canals in the great delta, we slept on an island, in a house built on stilts in the reeds, and cockerels crowed all through the night, and in Ho Chi Minh City, as Saigon is called now, we stayed at an old colonial hotel next to the river. We lunched on the roof terrace, papaya, mango, and dragon fruit, and something else, the name of which escapes me, perched on tall stools at a small, round table, and from there we could look out on the river, which had barely any water in it, the banks strewn with rubbish, and we'd sit in the constant din of mopeds and motor-bikes, blaring horns and the smell of exhaust fumes, there was no peace in the city, it wasn't at all anymore like you'd imagine it reading *The Ravishing of Lol Stein*, in which they go for drives in the evenings as the sun goes down and you see in your mind's eye a shiny black convertible with the top down, the white-clad women inside, gloves and hats and scarves, a seamless, gliding motion through the landscape. It wasn't like that at all, but it was nice anyway, and you discover we can take a bus to Cholon, the quarter where the eponymous Chinese-Vietnamese man in *The Lover* lives, there's a Chinese market there, the guidebook says. But when we get there, we realize straight away it's as impossible to imagine Duras in the Cholon of today as it is in the city itself. We visit a temple where we each write down a prayer on a little piece of red paper, after which they're attached to the inside of a spiral of coiled incense and the monk then sets the incense alight, the coil glows at the bottom as it burns, and he hoists it up under the roof where it remains suspended, smoldering with the other spirals, the glow gradually winding its way towards the prayers we've written. I don't know what you put in yours. I didn't tell you what I put in mine either. I don't recall the exact words I used, but I know that I asked for love and that I was thinking of us.

There, before we catch the bus back that evening, as darkness descends, we buy a folding metal table like the ones we sit at every night, three orange beakers made of plastic, and a heavy-duty sack to put the table in when we fly home. That table stands in front of our sofa now. I move the book that's on it and put your plate down in its place. The IKEA version was something we discovered in their outdoor furniture collection the following summer. We bought two, so now we've got three.

I shout to say that lunch is ready, you say you'll be with me in a minute. What you mean is that you must wait until your medication has dissolved. You're lying on the bed with the little white pill under your tongue. You say it's like submerging, the way the morphine spreads through your body and mellows you out. You take your painkillers before every meal, because when they removed the tumor they also had to cut away parts of your stomach, the whole of your spleen and a section of colon, and afterwards they sewed you back together again, but still, nearly eighteen months on, eating remains strenuous for you, which is why the pain specialist suggested morphine just before mealtimes, and it helps.

You have a pain specialist, a cancer specialist, a consultant and your own GP. Ti amo, you say, as you come in and sit down beside me on the sofa to eat. Now and then, you close your eyes, fork still in hand, and are gone for a moment, then to snap back again with a jolt, and you look at me as if you're afraid I noticed. After eating, you lean back into the sofa and I can see your face has taken on a more jaundiced hue, sicklier than before, I think I remember reading that it means the liver is failing, the cancer cells spreading inside it, but the thought of making a search and reading things through again exhausts me. The average life expectancy after the operation is fifteen to twenty months. We're at fifteen months now. I don't want to lose you, I sometimes find myself saying. I can say that, because it's something I could say before as well. I don't want to lose you. And tears well in my eyes, and I know that you see them, but we don't talk about death. You're not going to lose me, you tell me then. Never, never, never.

But I am already losing you. There's not much time left. It's what the cancer specialist said when I asked him, the moment you were out of the room the last time you had your chemo. It was between Christmas and New Year, and the doctor came in to say something to you, only you'd just gone out, I was on my own and finally able to ask without you listening. Can you tell me? I ask. Just me. You mean, how long? Yes. Can you just tell me? And he looks at me, young and handsome with long, dark curls and wide, earnest eyes, in his white coat. He looks like a shepherd boy in the Bible, from meadows outside Bethlehem. A year at the most, he says, no more than that. What does that mean? Three months? Maybe six, he says, but not a year. Not a year? Is that from today? Yes, from today, he says, and I've no longer any idea what we're doing, all I know is that I need to know something, something firm and of substance, even if it's when I can expect you to be dead. I need him to tell me, to give me a straight answer, give it to me, tell me, instead of all this avoidance, this mealy-mouthed pretense. But don't tell him, the doctor says, and fixes me with his big, brown eyes, stepping closer, standing right in front of me and lowering his voice. He needs hope, something to cling to, he explains in rapid Italian, so fast that all I can do is nod and say, yes, thank you, and a second later he's gone.

You want me to throw a party at ours on New Year's Eve. We had one in the old apartment, the first time there was a new year for us to enter together, I was in Oslo over Christmas seeing family and you were in Milan with your elderly mother and a sister-in-law widowed when your brother died, but I came back in good time for us to clean the place up and do the shopping and get things ready. You were so happy, we were both so happy, and I remember you standing preparing the food, in that big, open kitchen, standing in the light from above the counter, chopping vegetables, meticulous and focused, you cut the white from each and every little cube of pre-chopped bacon before frying them in the pan, and you were doing it for me so there'd be as little fat as possible in the salad, and having so many different salads was something you'd decided too, for my sake. In total, perhaps thirty people came, all, with the exception of a friend from Oslo, people you work with, some with kids, one couple with a dog, a well-known judge and his journalist wife, and Ciro who's a historian but makes his living writing about food, and he looks like it too, his lips are big and fleshy, it's as if he's always smacking his lips and tasting something even when he's talking, and his stomach is big and round, with a white shirt tucked in and suspenders to keep his trousers up. I was wearing a sequined dress and high heels, and this was before I'd learned to speak Italian, I'd only been living with you for three months, and even though in Italy people don't usually make speeches at parties, not even to bid everyone welcome once they've all arrived, things always being left to find their own fluency and fluidity, people standing around the room or seated on chairs that are pulled up as required or on the sofa up against the wall in the corner, but on our first New Year's Eve together I stood up on a stool and pinged my glass for attention and we all gathered around the kitchen table, everyone took turns to introduce themselves, in English, to each other, and to me, who barely knew anyone, everyone saying their name and a few words about what they did, and what their children were called, and the dog was called Caesar, and you were so proud of me, you looked at me and your eyes shone, I think you were happy, not only because I was standing up and making myself known, but also because I was trying to make a circle of your friends, to look at them, each and every one, and reach out to them, and because I was so clearly letting everyone see that I was here now, that now I was yours, I had come here to join you in this circle, this whole connection of people, the lives that surrounded yours, and was showing everyone that I wanted so deeply to be included in it and to belong.

Not a year left. It's the day before New Year's Eve and I'm still standing where I stood when I spoke to the doctor, at the foot of the bed in the little treatment room on the seventh floor of the National Cancer Institute on the Via Venezian, not far from the Piazza Piola, when you come back in, and I look at you and I can't tell you. And you smile at me, your head so small and odd-looking now, like that of a dithering old family member no one quite knows what to do with anymore, you sit down on the edge of the bed, it's just before noon, we're waiting for the chemo to arrive so the little bag can be hung up on the stand and the catheter can be inserted into the digital port you've had implanted under the skin of your chest, and the infusion can begin. Why can't they tell you? Why don't you want to know? You want us to throw a party this New Year's too. Tomorrow. It'll be our fourth New Year's Eve together. The first was when we gave the party in the old apartment, the second was in Oslo at a friend of mine's, drunk and full of joy we walked back through the snow from Grünerløkka, across the river and up the Telthusbakken, along St. Hanshaugen, up and over the final hill, past the park they call Idioten, until we were home. The third was last year here in Milan, we'd only just moved into the apartment high above the Darsena, such a view, the canal basin and all the traffic, the people and the noise, it was three months after your surgery, we were still in shock and your body was struggling to be a joined-up system again, you were in pain and frightened, and it was dark the whole time, the apartment a clutter of removal boxes, because we had no storage at that point, nowhere to put anything, your skinny body with the long, bumpy surgical scar all the way down your abdomen as you lay on your side on a towel on the fine new bathroom floor and the way you let me help you then, those nights when you were constipated and I would raise your soft bottom and locate your anus and carefully insert the long tube I'd warmed up in the bidet and greased with olive oil into your wrinkled hole and gently work it in as far as it would go and then squeeze the red rubber bulb to inject the lukewarm, oil-based solution as far as possible into your colon. The wave of your hand to tell me it's enough, Basta, basta, and I withdraw the tube and put it down in the bidet, there's excrement everywhere, and as you get to your feet I leave the room and close the door and stand and wait in the corridor, leaving you on your own in the bathroom, I listen and hope, as happy as you when it works, when something comes out, when all the hardness that pains you so much releases and is evacuated. Or else you've got diarrhea, and one morning you fall as you're about to sit down on the toilet, the little guest toilet behind the kitchen, it's all new in there, the pale, rose-colored tiles on the walls and the geometric pattern on the floor, we're so pleased we chose that especially, playful and elegant I think you'd have said, and it's early in the morning and my head is spinning from last night's wine, I drink myself into a stupor every night now that you're ill, drink myself away from it all, then collapse into bed, deep into sleep I drift, and from the depths of that sleep, in the early morning, I hear you calling out to me, your feeble voice, and I stagger into the kitchen. I've had an accident, you say from behind the door, and I'm standing there in my pajamas and don't dare look inside at first, scared to death that you've hurt yourself, that something serious has happened, that you've come apart even more, and the light is so bright inside that little room, but all I can do is go in, and there in the corner I find you on the floor where you've fallen, your hands covered in light-brown liquid excrement, your pajama bottoms soiled at the calves, it glistens on the floor where you're crumpled, on the toilet itself, and has sprayed up the walls. You're not hurt, you tell me, and I'm so relieved I begin to laugh, Poor you, I say, and you start to cry, because you're relieved too, you were scared I'd be angry with you.

It's now, with you wanting to have a party for New Year's, that I get angry. You aired the idea a couple of weeks before Christmas, said you'd like to throw a party, but we've hardly discussed it since then at all, you've got so little energy and in the evenings you're often out of sorts, and if occasionally we have guests over, you have to disappear off into the bedroom after a while and rest for a bit, so I think to myself it's just a thought that wafts by you every now and then, to throw a party, I suppose because you want everything to be the same as before, for everything to be light and buoyant, and of course I can understand that, only it's not the way things are and so I don't think anything will come of it, I assume you're grounded enough to realize. But then, the Saturday before Christmas, at an afternoon party at my friend's, my bridesmaid, who lives in this huge apartment and mixes with such a wide circle, and both of whose grown-up children are there, and their friends and some other people too, a writer we've met a few times and his wife, they smile the whole time and are both so vibrant, we're standing there with our proseccos in front of a table resplendent with olives and panettoni and little bruschette with different sorts of prosciutto, and you invite them to a New Year's party at ours. I sense it at once, my reluctance, but keep it to myself. They thank us and say they're not sure yet if they'll be able to come, they're planning a trip into the mountains with their little daughter and her grandparents and are looking forward to the break (he's just finished a novel called *Everywhere the Child*) and they're probably going to be there until after New Year's, but if they do decide to come back to the city before that, they promise to let us know. You invite my friend too, and her new boyfriend, and they don't know if they'll be able to come yet either, and it makes me think then that we can let it pass, that it's not like we've agreed to anything and set the ball rolling. And after that we go to Oslo and are there from the day before Christmas Eve until Boxing Day, you sleep on the sofa the whole time apart from when we're celebrating Christmas at my brother's and the day after at my dad's, and on Boxing Day we get up very early and catch the tram to the main station in the cold, and the train from there to the airport. You lie on the sofa in Oslo with a blanket over you, the standard lamp shining down on your head, it's dark outside, or else the sky is all colors in the transitions of the sun rising and setting, I watch you from the other sofa or the kitchen, you lie there with the iPad in your hands, reading, but then it's as if sleep simply wipes you out, it comes so gently, you're holding the iPad, but then your jaw drops and you're away, and it looks so very frail then, the life in you.

Then we're back in Milan and we're having this party, and all of a sudden you've invited another writer, someone I've also met, he's good fun, and his wife, they can come, and Ciro, the gourmand. That means there'll be five of us, assuming the others can't come. I don't want a party, but five is manageable, I can cope with five if it's so important to you, but the next evening a friend from Rome comes by with her husband and their three daughters, I barely know her, she's a journalist and does podcasts for RAI and is open and direct and engaging, I like her very much, it's the first time I've seen her kids, three lively girls who pitch in with their own stories, and we've bought apple juice and cookies, and the grown-ups are drinking wine, I'm looking after everyone's glasses and keeping the conversation going, and bringing and fetching and topping up, and listening to what's being said, and then when the medication has melted under your tongue you come into the living room and sit down like them on one of the orange stools, to join in and be a part of it all. A couple of hours later when they're getting ready to go and I'm feeling dazed and reeling from such an eddying confusion at such close quarters, of arms and legs and eyes and lives in motion, when my friend gets to her feet and they go out into the hall, to the great pile of sweaters and coats and scarves and hats that have been dumped there, you ask them then if they'd like to come over, them as well, for New Year's Eve. But we're here with a couple we know, my friend says, they have two children with them, and she smiles and raises an eyebrow in a beseeching question, and you say Great, fantastic, the more the merrier. I say nothing. I feel only resistance, only I don't know then what it is, or where it comes from. And after that they leave, my friend and her husband

and their daughters, and you go and lie down again while I clear things off to the kitchen.

Why can't we speak the truth? Why can't we say things the way they are? Why do they have to hide your death from you? Do you really not want to know, not be in contact with, not feel, the truth about yourself?

Today is Wednesday, January 8, and when I got back from the gym just before twelve you were getting dressed. All I do is sleep, you say, I never get out. And I sat down on the floor in my sweaty gym clothes in front of the bed you were sitting on the edge of, putting your socks on, those long, knee-length stockings gentlemen wear in Italy, and I looked at your face, which has become so wrinkled, and yet still it's you, still these are your eyes, and I feel as if I've come home when I look into your eyes. The way I look into your eyes and at the same time, always, know that you're going to die. It's been you and me and death for so long now. Although in a way it's just you, with me and death on the other side, because we don't talk about death. I can't understand how you can manage not to talk about it. I can only believe that somewhere inside you you do think about it. Are you not talking about it for my sake? It leaves us each alone with it.

I write *still it's you, still these are your eyes*. But is it still you, the person I see in those eyes? You're so medicated, your eyes aren't the same anymore, the look in them isn't the same, the place I found in them is gone in a way, that vast place that was there when I first met you, before you became ill, or our places, the places inside us, because I assume that's how it felt to you too, that we wandered through each other's inner places together, in each other's eyes. That we were a home to each other, there. But your eyes now are as if stiffened, they have no depth anymore, as if they're no longer in touch with anything inside you, or there's no opening in them that will allow me to slip inside. It's no longer home to me, to look into your eyes. They're just there.

I'm sitting here writing and you went out shortly before twelve, now it's ten past three and I hear your key in the door, you're home again. Hi, I call out, and you come in with your coat still on, straight into the study, and I get up from the computer and step towards you and kiss you on the mouth. So lovely to see you, you say with a smile, and I know you mean it with all your heart, but you're not feeling well, I can tell. I'm freezing, you say, it's warm in here, but the office was so cold. You're in pain, but the pharmacy was still waiting for your morphine pills to come in, you popped in there on your way home, but you say you've got something else you can take instead, you go into the bedroom and lie down, I want to fetch you a blanket, but you don't want one, and I can see there's something about your eyes, a darkness, I ask what you're thinking, standing beside the bed, smoothing my hand over your knee, is there something on your mind, I ask, meaning death, can we talk about death, only with a nod you indicate the briefcase you've left on the floor, the book I'm reading, you say, I was thinking about that.

And I've written fourteen novels, and if there's one thing my writing has to be, for me, it has to be truthful. What I write has to be truthful. I've wanted that to apply to my whole life too, in my relationships with other people, my relationship with myself. I broke off with my mother for two years, three months and four days when I was about thirty, because I couldn't feel myself when she was around or when I spoke to her on the phone. All I could feel then was her. Or the person I thought was her, what she was inside me, regardless, I no longer knew what I felt inside. It was either me or her. And so I broke off with her, because I needed to be with myself first. To grow strong inside so I didn't disappear when she was around. All those counseling sessions, all those body treatments and all that meditation and analyzing my dreams. Carl Gustav Jung said somewhere that all we can hope for on our journey through life is an ego strong enough to endure the truth about ourselves. And I'm under no illusion that I see the full and complete truth about myself, but one thing I do know is that I have a compulsion for truth that feels like my very life force itself. And that it makes me ill when I go against that force, when I go against myself.

How ill I was that New Year's Eve. It started the evening before, when I submitted to holding a party the way you wanted it, with all the children and everything, when we took the red wheelie shopper and went out to buy what we needed, it was late, but everything's open late here, you'd had your chemo in the afternoon, it was December 30, the same day the doctor stepped closer to me and said, Not a year from today, which meant that it was our last December 30 and would be our last New Year's Eve too, and you wanted us to throw a party for nine adults and five children, you, so steeped in chemo and morphine, and I, so exhausted from being by your side in all this, from doing everything on my own, because you've so little energy. You want us to spend our last New Year's Eve making food for people we hardly even know, or don't know at all, people who don't have death on their minds every single minute of the day, for whom New Year's Eve is all about fireworks and champagne and looking gleefully ahead into the future. But we have no future to celebrate! Don't you get it? I can't throw a party without truth. But I didn't tell you that. You insisted on a party. It was so important to you, that party. And I was angry with you for being so insensitive to the situation, for not tuning in to how I felt. What's this party all about? You couldn't answer me that, not properly. It's for you, you said.

And on New Year's Eve I woke up with a temperature,

phlegmy and coughing, I sat down on the sofa with you in the morning knowing that I could choose to go back to bed, like you, only I didn't, it really felt like there was a choice I had to make and that it was crucial, and after a minute I erred in the opposite direction, got to my feet and got started, slowly working my way through the day, systematically preparing the food, the things that could be done well in advance, the things that couldn't and had to wait, I brought our Vietnam stools in and washed them down, got the living room ready, put tea lights out, and fat candles, organized a table for drinks and glasses, set out the plates and cutlery, and napkins, bowls of clementines, chips, and olives. We'd told everyone half past eight, but Ciro came early, with his suspenders stretched tight over his shirt and a magnum of champagne that we put outside to chill on the balcony, only he left again just after ten, the bottle's still on the floor in the hall, but before he went I sat down with him on the sofa for a bit, Ciro with his big belly, he asked me to, Come here, he said, and patted the cushion beside him, he was the one I knew best out of everyone there, and he told me about the two women he was seeing, coincidentally they had the same name, which was practical, he said, and we laughed, and then he lowered his voice to a whisper and said it's hard for the one who's ill, but much worse in a way for the one who isn't, and that's when I teared up, I don't care who it's worse for, it's just so seldom anyone ever talks to me or asks how I am, and when everyone arrived at half past eight I sat down on a stool in the kitchen with a huge gin and tonic and my phone and wouldn't speak to anyone, I was ill, and they could tell from my voice that I was, but mostly I was angry, or else I was so angry it made me ill, for not saying I was angry, but anyway I sat there for a whole hour on my own.

And you were okay with that, you weren't angry about me being angry, because I make you happy, you always say so, that I make you so happy the way I am, so me needing to sit on my own in the kitchen was something you respected and supported, you were on my side, you give me space, always, and it's up to me to find out what's good for me and draw a line. I make you so happy. As you make me happy, which was why I wanted to throw that party even though I didn't want to. I did it for you.

Maybe I should have gone at things differently from the start. But in a way it's as if everything hangs together, from long before you got ill, from right back when we first met. We're so different in the way we relate to the world, in what's good for us. Your equivocation, for instance. You say you love me, and in everything you've ever done you've always shown me you do, you want me with you wherever you go, on your business trips, yet it always felt like there was a hesitancy there, that somehow you weren't going all in and that everything came with a certain reservation or uncertainty that perhaps wasn't to do with us at all, but with you, or perhaps it is you, the way you are, a person who hesitates and waits and sees, but whatever it was it played on my deep unrest as to whether you actually, really wanted me. That's how it was with our sex too, you indulged, yet often it felt like you stopped being a part of it, as if you pulled back halfway through instead of pressing closer. When we talked about it, when I said I wondered if there was an intensity between us that we weren't releasing, which I felt was missing, you said at first that you considered it was just a matter of time, that we'd get there further down the line. But then not so long ago, when we talked about it again – and now talk is all we do, because we don't have sex anymore since you became ill, it's as if everything's dead down there, you said, indicating your limp dick as we sat in bed one night, your penis, once such a fine cock, looks quite forlorn now beneath the long scar from the surgery, when they clawed so much out of you it left a hollow – you said you weren't sure if there actually was anything more, anything stronger in you, further down the line. That maybe there just wasn't anything wilder in the person you were, you said, that you think that's probably just the way sex is, for you.

And it was such a relief when you told me, because I began to think then that the idea of intensity was perhaps just another of our porn-infected illusions, the videos, all those images of panting, perspiring, high-powered sex, the wanting and taking, the moaning and groaning, the slapping of flesh and screaming, and maybe the idea of there being some kind of release in that was just an illusion too, that the promise of the boundary-pushing encounter, and the release it would give, the belief that there would be something there, which had made me feel a sorrow of sorts for our not having embarked on finding that place together, maybe that place didn't exist.

Why can't we talk about you dying? In that, too, we're far apart. I think it's possible to give ourselves up to each other and go new places together in sex too, but it would take tenacity. Is that what's missing, tenacity? What can I do for you now? How can a person give tenacity to someone? When that other person doesn't want tenacity and would prefer not to relate to the fact that he's dying. I can't force it on you. I can't force you. I can't press death into your face like a pillow. All I can do is be here, beside you.

Are you in your pictures? You're a publisher, that's how we met, you publish my books in Italian. But when you were young you wanted to be an artist, you wanted to paint, and you went to art schools in the US and Paris, that's what you're trained as, you didn't study literature. And you carried on with your painting when you came back to Milan, your mother supported you, she bought you a two-room apartment where you set up a studio, that's where you painted, and sometime when you were in your twenties you had your own exhibition, landscapes on copper plate, they gleam like gold from the copper underneath. A single exhibition, and when it was over the woman you were married to at the time said that was enough, it was time you joined the publishing house, held down a proper job and earned some money. And your father, who had founded the publishing house and was held in such high esteem, a cultivated gentleman as they say, whose interests lay in art and design and antique Chinese furniture and prints, he never hung a single one of your pictures in that huge apartment. As a painter you meant nothing to him. And you stopped painting. The studio was rented out to a student. You're an intelligent, sensitive man, and you made a good publisher, you read Harry Potter and enthused about it, long before it was a thing, and you've published Astrid Lindgren and Žižek and Jung, *The Red Book*, you've got good Italian authors, and between you you've built up a flourishing house with a host of imprints all with their various focus areas, you've even started a very strong small publishing house in Spain.

In a way, we've opposing stories, I wanted to be a psychologist and scholar, but then in a waiting period I started writing and at the same time fell in love with a writer and he helped me to believe it would work out for me, that it was actually possible to make writing the most important thing in my life. I found support. You didn't. But I think I went looking for that support. I went to someone who some part of me must have known would help me live the life I needed to live in order to grow. How was I able to do that? I went looking for the support I needed, found it and have been writing ever since. Whereas you sought support in someone who only made you give up what was yours.

When we first met, you carried a notebook whose closely spaced lines you filled with tiny handwriting. You told me you were writing a novel about a young woman, I think she was sitting in a tree or something. And you wrote music, sequences of music that kept appearing in your mind, compositions that were more advanced than you were capable of playing your-self on the piano, a young pianist would sometimes come and give you lessons, he studied those pieces with you and played parts of them so that you could hear what it was you'd written.

But you'd already heard them inside you. I thought it was so brilliant you being able to hear these structures of sound inside you, visible only when turned into lines of notes on a computer, to me it was totally abstract, I couldn't hear a thing. You were always working on something or other, it was a need you had, to create things. And when I asked you, when I came to live with you in Milan more than three years ago, why you didn't take up your painting again, you answered me rather vaguely to begin with and said only that it was all a bit difficult. And so many things are convoluted and unnecessarily laborious in Italy, you get the feeling the systems are designed to make you give up before you've even started, there are so many regulations, so much red tape and hardly anything can be done online from home, you've got to get up in the morning and go there, take a number and sit in great big rooms for hours on end with hordes of people on clapped-out plastic chairs, to get done whatever it is you need to get done. It was difficult, you said, because your studio was rented out and the young guy who was living there had an eight-year lease with three years still to go. You could phone him and talk to him about it, I suggested. And eventually you did, and doubtless because you'd been so generous and let him live there at the lowest possible rent, because of course there are regulations for that as well, upper and lower limits, he agreed, and a couple of months later he phoned and said he'd found somewhere else and could now move out. From that day on, you were at the studio every Saturday and Sunday, and during the week you'd sometimes be there for a couple of hours over lunch, or in the afternoons if you had no meetings to go to at work.

Imagining the pictures you were working on filled me with excitement. Would they show me who you were inside, give me a point of entry into places in you I'd never been? Places I hoped and believed really did exist, that was the reason I fell for you in the first place, your eyes, the promise they held of this great inner landscape where perhaps I could wander too, at your side. Who are you?

Did you stop painting because you stopped believing? Believing in yourself, that what you were doing was worth it, that your work and what you could offer, the person you were then, was important enough to build a life around? But to give up painting is also to give up seeing. To give up looking inwards, into your self.

The first pictures you did were of animals. Four big canvases with a lion in them, and one with a rabbit. Besides the main figures in those works, you were concerned too with embellishment, it was the start of something that was to become much more prominent, your interest in ornamentation, much the same way as Bonnard works too, with light, for instance, the way the light reflects in the tiling of a bathroom where a woman reclines naked in a bathtub, the way light falling on a surface can possess a meaning all its own. I wondered where you were in those paintings. Were you the lion? And what were those candles in the background, burning with such small flames? Were you in their bold colors? These were helpless pictures, even I could see that. You'd stopped painting thirty years ago, and it was as if you needed to loop backwards and come at it again from behind in order to rediscover yourself there and get started again. But after that it all took off so quickly, since then you've progressed series by series, but although each new series has been a departure and moved you forward in that way, I think it's probably more the skill side of things where you've improved, rather than what your pictures actually express. Technically, you're very proficient. But what are you trying to do in your paintings, if they don't capture something *more* than the actual motif? The ones I feel have the strongest contact with an emotion are those belonging to a series of self-portraits you did. At last I could see you. You painted five in all, and in each case an extra little picture has been attached, a kind of accoutrement, a shadow of something internal to the main picture, or perhaps a comment on it. So you can actually look at the picture as a whole and think: What if the little one wasn't there? What if the main picture was the only thing that was shown or said or seen? What would that have been like? Because each of the small pictures does something other than the big one to which it belongs, they bring in a different quality, a sense of displacement, presenting the prospect of something more, something beyond what seems possible in the main picture.

I've persuaded you to bring one of them home, the one I like best, it hangs here now in the hall. It's your face, painted with bold strokes, and it's as if you're not quite there, as if the figure that's you is somehow at a loss, your expression one of despair, in blue and green, and a bird casts a dark shadow in the background. In the small picture that's screwed into the top right of the main frame, everything changes. The hue is pale red, a light is coming, and there, there the bird flies.

It's a long time since you were last at the studio. It's on the third floor, with no lift, and the stairs make you dizzy. It's a twenty-minute walk from here. You haven't the strength. If you feel you've got some, you go to the office instead.

We don't talk about it, even though I think it must be another reason you don't go to the studio anymore. That in order to produce something, you need the energy to sense what's there. To feel yourself close to it. Take warmth from it, as Trotzig writes, exploit it, put it back into the work. Not necessarily as a motif, but the force that's in it, that force is what's you in the now, and no matter what else is true, that's what's going to be there to be seen and felt, in the work.

And if you won't think about dying. If you don't want to know. But something in you must know. And use up so much energy not wanting to know. How are you supposed to paint then?

When I met you first, when I saw you there in your light-colored suit jacket and your light-colored slacks, with your straggly white hair, when you came into the hotel foyer with a group of foreign publishers and shone in the middle of the group, even then, and when I spoke to you the next day, when you stepped out onto the stairs to have a smoke and we talked about Venice and I was embarrassed because I love Venice so much, and it made you smile, and you said that you found Venice extremely beautiful too, even then there was something about you that made me think of Mr. Lilyvale. Astrid Lindgren's Mr. Lilyvale, who taps his knuckle on the window of little Goran who lies ill in his bed, who takes Goran out with him, takes him by the hand and whisks him away in that hour of the evening when twilight falls, which is how Goran is introduced to the Land of Twilight. So that he may prepare himself for death. It was as if there was something of Lilyvale about you even then, from the very start. It scares me sometimes, that we can know things with such certainty, see them and think them, and what's scary is not the fact that this is so, because that's just the way it is, what's scary is that it's only afterwards that we, or I, take it seriously. But perhaps that's also because we don't know what it is that we see, what it means. What was it I saw in you that made me think of Mr. Lilyvale? Did I see even then that you carried a nearness to death inside you? Because there's something about you that, in a way, is outside of time. As if you're actually an old man, something dusty and old-fashioned about you that I've always liked. And at the same time you're not that at all, you're only eight years older than me, and much savvier, for instance, when it comes to phone apps and the like, and whereas I can barely bend my body, you're as supple as a yogi. But that was one of the feelings I had about you, and which I've had all along. That there was a Mr. Lilyvale in you. So maybe it's me who's Goran, and you're here to show me that death exists. I, who have toiled and toiled to find an entry into life, to live and to feel, I've always thought there was something contrived about it when people go on about being so sensitive to death, being afraid of death. How can they, I've always wondered, these living people? I've struggled so hard just to feel the heart beating in my chest, to feel there's something there that's alive inside me, and not just steel and stone. Death would come all in good time. And then you came.

I look out the window facing the rear courtyard and notice that behind the dome of San Lorenzo you can actually see the uppermost spire of the Duomo. I check my phone, there's a text from you, you're at the publishing house, it's Friday, January 9 and the time is 15:45, and you're asking if the pharmacy's got anything for you yet, you still haven't managed to get hold of anyone at the hospital. Shit. I forgot all about the pharmacy when I was out earlier, we agreed this morning that I'd go there about lunchtime and ask if your medication had come.

It's your morphine you're asking about, you take 200 micrograms of Fentanyl to take the top off the pain, and besides that the patches for your shoulder, they give out 150 micrograms an hour, we change them every 72 hours.

Yesterday you stayed home from the office, you were having such pain, and I went to the pharmacy for you in the morning, but there was nothing on the way just yet, they said.

In the afternoon, after I'd finished writing, you got dressed and I went with you to your GP, her surgery's by the park in the Solari district and we walked there as the sun was setting, the sky all pinks and oranges, the way it so often is at that time of day now in winter. Hearing that someone was in with her, we waited in the narrow corridor outside her door, you'd already phoned in the morning and all we were there for was to pick up a prescription. You sat down on a chair while I wandered back and forth looking at the posters and notices, one of which I read in its entirety, an ad for a new local counseling service, three sessions for free, it said, underlined in blue. If only that was all it took, I thought, and then it was your turn and you went in to get the prescription for the tablets the pharmacy had already released to you in advance, and because you didn't close the door properly I heard her ask, How are you doing? and your reply, Not so good at the moment, only she didn't agree with that, I think you're looking much better, she said, and you thanked her then for the prescription, See you soon, you said, and came back out to where I was waiting. Your little head under your felt hat, and your eyes, big and grey in your slightly pudgy face, swollen with cortisone.

When we left the surgery you said you felt like a cup of hot chocolate, so we walked to Clivati i Viale Coni Zugna and you ordered one with whipped cream and a cup of coffee for me and you remained standing over at the counter with your back to me in your navy blue North Face coat you told me you bought years ago for a business trip some of you took to a publisher in northern China where the temperature could drop to below minus thirty-five. The hood hung down between your shoulders and you had your hat on and looked like a little boy in front of the tall marble counter where you dipped into the cream and spooned it into your mouth as soon as it came, as if everything else in the world ceased to exist at once.

From there we went to the pharmacy again, the people who work there are all young, with scarves around their necks and thermal coats on top of their normal white pharmacy coats because the automatic doors have got stuck and won't close, all from the South, from Sicily or Naples, you say you can tell from the way they talk, which I can't, but they're all very nice and would bend over backwards to help you, and as we came through the door I felt you tense up, a tiny contraction of hope, but then when we got to the glass counter and there still wasn't any morphine for you, you sank, you looked at me, and for a moment your face was quite desolate and unsavable, you handed them the prescription from your GP, for the medication you'd already received, and then we walked home. You lie down on the bed when we get in, but after only a short while I hear you rush to the loo, the hot chocolate seems to go right through you, and when you've finished you go straight back to the bedroom to lie down again. You whimper. You're in such pain. I hover in the doorway and say you must phone the hospital. It's evening, soon it'll be night, and you can't lie here in pain like this. If your GP won't help, and the pharmacy can't get you your medication, the hospital will have to do something. You need attention, I say. And so you phone the hospital and ask to be put through to the doctor who's responsible for you, it's just after seven o'clock and dark outside, but they're still on the job, and she comes to the phone, the doctor with the long henna-dyed hair and horn-rimmed glasses, the one who lisps when she speaks, sometimes she's wearing frayed jeans with embroidered flowers on them under her open coat, and purple or pink anatomically shaped shoes, she's like a little girl, a little girl who wants to be somewhere else, I think every time she comes into the treatment room when you've had your chemo and are waiting to go home, while I'm lying on the blue synthetic leather sofa next to you reading. It's as if she never has time for us then, as if all she can do is drop off your discharge summary with the updated details of your treatment, another entry with each appointment, and then leave again, for somewhere far away, as quickly as she can. Arrivederci, she said, and had already turned on her heels when I stopped her – this was the time before last, in mid-December, you go every two weeks – Excuse me, I'd just like to know how things are progressing, I said. What do the tests say? She knows I mean the CA 19-9 marker tests, and says obscurely that yes, they've gone up a bit, but it's hard to tell the reason, it could be infections, it could be something else, it's nothing to worry about until the next scan, she says, and with a quick smile she's gone again. The scan she mentioned is on Monday.

When we got home from the hospital that time in mid-December, I found the discharge summary on the desk in the bedroom and turned it over and read your record then from the bottom up, it was the first time I'd read it myself, and why hadn't I done so before, it was all there in black and white.

Now all the hennaed doctor can do is advise you to phone the pain specialist. You thank her and wish her a good evening, then make the call right away, only to discover office hours there are between nine in the morning and four pm, there's no one to answer the phone in the evenings. But you're in such pain. Can't we put another patch on, I suggest. The Fentanyl patches are the only thing you've got. So that's what we do, we give you another 50 micrograms, then another 50 on top of that, and at last, after being racked with pain, in agony all through the day, at last you fall asleep.

That was yesterday.

This morning we gave you another 100, so now you've got three hundred and fifty micrograms of morphine an hour discharging into you through your skin, and then, after a night sitting bent double or twisting and turning, you nevertheless get up, as if your will was a completely different body inside your own, you get up and stand on your feet and somehow, improbably, manage to propel yourself to the office.

What your record said was that since the end of October your markers have doubled with every test. Reading backwards, I could see this was a new development. In the year you've been having chemo after the surgery, your numbers have been up and down, but have never exceeded four thousand. At the end of November you were up to five thousand and something. By mid-December it was over ten. They run the test after every other session, but they didn't on December 30, there's no CA 19-9 in the record for that date. Yet the pain you're in increases every day, every night, and now you've got this swelling. It's Friday night. Monday, when you're due in next, is three days away.

After visiting your GP, on our way to the Clivati pasticceria, we stop at a pet shop and go inside, passing between the aquariums, walls of glass behind which little fish dart, red and yellow, so quick they are, so much movement, so dainty and graceful, so much life. We want suet cakes, feed to put out for the birds on the balcony. We go up to the counter at the back of the shop, there's another customer before us, a woman with two small white poodles, one of which yaps at you fiercely, I step back, but it doesn't frighten you, you smile and crouch down to give it a pat, and there's another dog too, behind the counter, a black labrador that wags its tail and comes towards you, and you pat that one too and ruffle its coat and talk to it, and the pet shop woman and the dog woman stand yakking away as if we didn't exist, and you seem so contented, crouching there with the dogs around you, but now I can speak so much Italian that I manage to get a word in and ask if we can buy some suet cakes for the birds, and the pet shop woman calls for her mother who's talking to some other people in the back room, where the labrador came from, I can see two more dogs asleep on a cushion there in the corner, and the mother comes out and you stand up straight again. Thanks, you say to me, I got distracted, and the mother asks how many suet cakes we want, you say they're usually gone in no time, so we buy ten. She puts them in a bag for us, you say goodbye to the dogs, and we carry on then to the pasticceria.

This morning I put two of the cakes out on the makeshift bird table you've cobbled together, the saucer from an empty terracotta pot, the pot upturned, the saucer balanced on top. On the street when we were out walking you found a stone you dropped into your pocket, you've placed it in the middle now to add some weight, and have scattered some sunflower seeds and sesame seeds. And now this is what we talk about in the mornings, sitting on the sofa in our pajamas with our coffee, though you don't drink coffee anymore, only tea, and a piece of panettone each. We watch the birds, their comings and goings, and you know the names of all the various kinds, you tell me what they're called in Italian. And we sit there looking out instead of at each other, we talk about them and are together in that, instead of in what we see when we look at each other and don't talk about.

Now it's Saturday, January 10, it's 14:44 and I've sat down to write, I'm writing every day now, following the same routine, we get up, I make coffee and tea, we have breakfast on the sofa, you go for a lie down and I read for a bit, then go to the gym and work out, I work out nearly two hours a day in the little gym on the Via Panzeri a bit further along from our building. I come home, shower, have lunch, on my own or with you, if you've stayed at home, as you have today. Then you go for a lie down again, while I lie for forty minutes on my back on the living-room floor with my legs up on the sofa at ninety degrees, I lie there and listen to a kind of music from a therapy cushion I ordered online from the U.S., it gives out music I select from a dedicated app on my phone, half the tracks are designed for people wth autism, and then there are ten that are soothing and therapeutic for people in general. I lie there and know that I'm going to write. I think about my writing, but mostly I'm just aware of my body, attentive to what's happening with it, sensing how my back flattens towards the floor, the way my mouth slowly opens as my jaw relaxes.

When you texted me yesterday to ask if the pharmacy had got anything for you yet, I was actually immersed in my writing. I just happened to pause for a minute and gaze out the window, and then I checked my phone even though I know it's a stupid thing to do, because I can get so easily distracted then, which was what happened yesterday, with you having texted me and me having forgotten. I didn't want to be the sort of person who forgets to go to the pharmacy for you, and since my attention was already elsewhere I decided immediately that I could just as well go out, down the stairs and along the street to find out, I wasn't going to get anymore writing done anyway, not before I'd gone to find out, and it's no use phoning them, because they don't know who I am unless they see me, and the medication we need is dope with a big red warning on it, the anesthesiologist who lives in the flat below mine in Oslo said back in August when we were there and you hadn't brought enough of your medication with you, or needed to take what you had, which I completely understand, but my anesthesiologist neighbor, who I phoned to ask if he could help us, or help you, and write out a prescription, he said it wasn't that easy, there was a special procedure, a safeguard of some kind that meant he couldn't access what you needed for a couple of days, because the tablets you're talking about, he said, are worth a fortune on the street. It was still light out, the sun was still shining, and it was nice to get some fresh air, I told myself as I went along the Viale Papiniano in the direction of the Corso

Genova and the pharmacy on the right-hand side there, just five minutes from where we live. And they know us there now, me as well as you, and when my turn came, the young woman behind the counter immediately checked her computer, they've got Fentanyl on order for you constantly, so if the main hub had got some in, it would already be on its way, that was what you were hoping I'd be able to tell you, that it was, only it still hadn't come. Four hundred micrograms, she says, peering into her screen, that's all they've got at the hub, two packets of four hundred, but he can split those in two, she says and looks up at me, your prescription's for two hundred. Yes, I say, brilliant, that's excellent. It's already four o'clock almost, so it's too late for tonight, she tells me, but they'll be here first thing in the morning. I ask her what time and she says half past eight and smiles a big smile, we're relieved, both of us are, and I thank her again and say I'll come back then, and I go back out into the light and dig out my phone and call you. The news makes you so happy. That's quicker than they could manage at the hospital, you tell me, because now they've finally got back to you. I love you, you say, more than anything in the world. And

I love you, I say, See you soon, and then we say Ciao and hang up and I go up the stairs to the sixth floor and into the study and carry on with what I was writing yesterday.

Today I'm writing this. It's Saturday. This morning after breakfast you got dressed and went to the pharmacy, I was lying on the sofa reading when you got back, the small birds have discovered the suet cakes we've put out for them and you think they'll like panettone as well, you gave them a piece of yours from your breakfast and they're still pecking away at it, I see them fluttering about in the corner of my eye as I read, and you come through the door with a whole different energy than you've had all week. How did it go, did you get two packets? I ask. No, only one, you say, and immediately I feel depleted, they couldn't even get you two packets, but you're pleased, you're happy, you're holding the packet in your hand as you hang up your coat and take off your shoes, I'm not the only one who needs this stuff in Milan, you say generously, because at this moment, you're holding an unopened packet with four super-sized white tablets in it. I'll take the first one whole, you say.

When I come to the bedroom doorway to say goodbye

shortly afterwards, I'm on my way to the gym, you're lying on your back with your head on the pillow, your knees drawn up and your eyes closed, and you look so peaceful. See you soon, I whisper, and glance back at you as I turn away, and you say Mm, with eyes still closed, and lift your hand almost imperceptibly in a wave. At last, I think.

Then when I come back you're like you were more than a month ago, happy, vibrant, you tell me it even helps your writing, the medication, the sci-fi crime novel you're writing on your phone, you haven't been able to work on it for several days this week, but now you've returned to it, and you talk for a long time on the phone while I slice the smoked salmon we brought back with us after Christmas, and some vegetables, making us a salad, it's a colleague of yours in Rome you're talking to, you've got some meetings lined up with him there in a couple of weeks and have planned the whole thing, booked the hotel from your bed, mapped out a trip for us, first to Rome for your work there, then a weekend in Naples, which I've always wanted to see, though until now we've never been. But increasingly I've been thinking it won't come to anything, this past week especially it's been looking quite inconceivable that a fortnight from now we could get on a train to go anywhere at all. Monday, the day after tomorrow, you're having your scan. But now, with 400 micrograms under your tongue, followed by a couple of hours' sleep, you're again so exquisite and smooth-featured, bright and buoyant, almost like new again.

Who are you? Are you the morphine man, or are you the man you've been all week while you've had no pills to take, the man in pain, increasing pain, afraid and turned inwards? What is the truth? Where are you? My dearest. Soon I'm going to lose you, but I don't know where you are while you're here either.

And who am I? I haven't yet mentioned A. I've been thinking I could write this without him becoming a part of it. That this is about you and me, and that I'll continue writing it until you die.

I write those words, *until you die*, and I start to cry, and I don't know where *I* am either. I wander through the days, knowing that you're dying, only somehow I can't feel it. It's ungraspable, that you're going to die. I don't know what it is. How it is. I don't know. For now, you're still here, and I can think the thought that you're going to die, I can force myself to imagine waking up with you no longer beside me in our bed, I can think about waiting for you to come into the living room and drink your breakfast tea with me, that one day you won't be coming in anymore, that one day you'll just be gone. I can try to *relate* to that. But for now that's not what's real. What's real is that you're still here, and at the same time, as if embedded in that, the fact that soon you're going to die. Often I don't feel a thing.

We've been through so many phases in the time you've been ill, but after we got married in the summer, you'd been ill for a year then, and for a long time it was as if everything was all about getting that done, getting married, as if that was our focal point, the thing we were moving towards instead of death, and we were going there together, but after we got married there was nothing ahead of us anymore, nothing we had to look forward to, together. All there is now is that you're going to die. And you say you're not. So we're not together in that, or at least it's not something we talk about, but still it's the point towards which we're heading now.

I've been feeling so very low. It feels like it's never going to be possible to ever feel happy again, buoyantly happy, the kind of happiness I used to know, in which the thought of death was quite absent. I think that from now on any happiness I feel will be tinged with death. Maybe for others it's always been like that and I've just been naïve. But happiness for me has always been so straightforward. Being happy in that way feels like not even being in the world anymore. And for a long time just looking at you was painful to me, I couldn't look at you without the knowledge that you're going to die, your eyes, everything about you said *death* to me. And even though it's not that acute anymore, it still won't pass, now it's quieter in a way, normal almost, death has become an attendant presence, everything's just the way it is, I'm here with you and soon you won't be here anymore.

A is a man I met in Mexico. I've been traveling quite a bit with work, book launches and readings, library events, literary festivals and university conferences in various places since the middle of September until this coming December 8. In between obligations I've been able to get back to Milan now and then, and whenever possible, whenever your chemo schedule has allowed, and when you've been feeling up to it, you've come with me. We were at the Frankfurt Book Fair together, where of course you had your own meetings to attend, the ones you felt you could manage, and just before that we spent a few days in Berlin, I had an event at a bookshop there, and from Frankfurt we went on to Düsseldorf and Zürich, to the Literaturhäuser, where I read from my work and you rested in the hotel room, you hadn't the energy, you had to choose between the event itself and going out with everyone afterwards, which was what we preferred, and in Zürich you met up with me and the women from the Literaturhaus just along the street from where we were staying, there was a pub with a kitchen that was open late and we had white sausage with sauerkraut, you even had a small beer. That was late October, and after that I was off on my travels again, to Ravenna, followed by a library tour that took me through the south of Norway, a book launch in the UK, with events in London, Norwich, and Edinburgh, intervals at home in Milan with you, and then that last trip before Christmas, after which everything was going to be quiet and I'd be staying put for three months, was at the beginning of December, to the book fair in Guadalajara, Mexico.

I'm so exhausted by all that traveling, so exhausted from being scared you won't hold out until I come home again, every time I've been home it's been to check and make sure you're still alive. When it started to dawn on me during the spring, how much traveling I'd be doing in the autumn, how intense it was going to be, two and a half months solid, that was all I could think about, how things were going to be with you. Were those trips even feasible? Normally I'd have looked forward to it, and no matter how strenuous it was going to be, I'd have enjoyed it like an adventure. Now it was all death and you, and the time we had left. All that traveling meant precious time we were never going to get back, our time together. But what kind of time would it have been if I'd just stayed at home and sat there watching death encroach upon your face. And you wanted me to go. Go, you said. I'll be fine. And so I went, and all I wanted was to come back. That whole autumn was like an archer's bow stretched taut: will you still be here when all this is done and at last I come home?

My final trip, I pack a carry-on suitcase for Mexico, a country I've never been to before, but you've attended the same book fair twice, and for a long time I thought you were going to come with me, that we could grab the chance, it's my last engagement, so we'd have time for ourselves afterwards, to see some more of the country, Mexico City, or perhaps travel out to the coast, and so I send off a few emails and look into things, though not with any real faith that it's going to happen, because you're getting weaker, but it's as if you can't feel it yourself, you really want to be well and be with me, to live life with me, to enjoy with me the life we so much love. A year ago, in January, I was at the book fair in Jaipur and you were meant to be there too, you were the one who'd encouraged me to wangle an invite, after we'd been to India together, Kolkata, Varanasi, and Mumbai, and we wanted to go back and if I got an invite we'd be able to go to Jaipur together, you as publisher, me with my books, and when the invitation came you bought a ticket too and so much wanted to go, but it was only three months after your surgery and you were still having trouble with your bowels, everything they'd cut away and sewn up, and then there was the chemo, you weren't used to it, it wiped you out completely, and so you ended up staying home. When I attended the Bay Area Book Festival in Berkeley five months later, in May, the kind organizer booked tickets for us both, a single reservation so we could sit together all the way, you wanted to go there too, but when the time came you didn't have the energy then either, so again I sat by myself on the flight and drank gin and tonics on my own, I sent you a photo of the hotel room when I got there, the room that was meant to have been ours, and we talked on the phone and I ordered takeaway every night from the Chipotle across the street and sat in my great big American window and ate my food and looked out at the traffic, with the time difference between us, you at home in bed in Milan, I thought about you asleep in our bed, and all the time, in everything I thought, you were going to die.

The email from the organizers in Mexico says it's hot in the daytime but cool in the evenings and inside with the air conditioning on, so I pack one sleeveless black dress and a black woollen top I can wear underneath, one jacket, tights, clean underwear for each day I'm going to be there, my running shoes and gym clothes. It all goes into my cabin bag so I won't have to hang around at the baggage carousels when I arrive back at Malpensa, you say you'll come and meet me, the way you always used to before you became ill, whenever I was away, you'd come all the way out to the airport on the shuttle train, because you don't have a driver's license, you could never wait for me at home, you always said, not if you had the chance to come and meet me, and that's what you're going to do this time as well, so if all I've got is a carry-on it means I can get off the plane, hurry along the corridors and go straight through baggage reclaim out into the arrivals hall, and at long, long last be done with all my travels and finally be home, home, home with you.

On the outbound journey there's a stopover in Madrid, it's evening and I drink a whole bottle of prosecco I bought at the airport in Milan, sitting by a window watching the planes as they move out onto the tarmac in the dark, talking to you on the phone, you're in your pajamas on your way to bed, and my flight departs at eleven-thirty, I find my seat and drink what comes with the food, until I fall asleep, which was the point of all the wine, all I want is to drink myself away. It's a little after three-thirty am when we land in Mexico City, mid-morning back home, the connecting flight leaves at seven, an hour is all it takes, and then I'll be in Guadalajara.

It's Sunday as I write this, Sunday, January 12, you're going into the hospital tomorrow and I'm going with you, we've set the alarm on your phone, yours plays a classical tune, and tonight, after I've finished writing, I'm going to pack a small suitcase for you, and one for me, because I'm going to be staying the night with a friend who lives near the hospital. I wonder what it's going to be like further down the line, if you're going to be in the hospital at the end, or if it'll happen suddenly, and if you're going to be in the hospital I'll be sleeping there too, at your bedside, the way I did for a whole fortnight when you had your surgery. I need to check if it's going to rain, I don't think so, the sun's out now, it's been unusually sunny this winter, normally winter in Milan means fog and drizzle, but at the moment it's clear and sunny, day after day, we're lucky. But I still need to check, because I've hung your clothes out to dry so they'll be ready for when Rosa comes while we're at the hospital tomorrow, Rosa from Peru, who comes in on Mondays and Fridays and does our washing for us and irons all our clothes, she stands in the kitchen listening to a Peruvian radio station, or else she chatters away on her phone with her kids in Spanish, she stands there after she's done the cleaning, ironing your boxers, your shirts, putting the creases in your slacks, she even irons our socks, my undies, the towels and the bed clothes, and every day after you've washed, there's a clean and ironed shirt for you to put on.

I go about here numbed, but lots of things are important to me, little things. Like our clothes, washing our clothes when the weather lets me hang them out on the line on the kitchen balcony, we still haven't figured anything out for drying them indoors, as we'd talked about. I like to see our clothes hanging there, I like hanging them out, picking them up, giving them a shake, pegging them on the line. I make sure there's yogurt for you in the fridge, and Chinotto, a sparkling soft drink you're fond of at the moment. I remember to put a glass of water out next to your tea in the mornings, for your antacids, and I stock up on risotto rice and Parmesan cheese so I can make *riso in bianco* for you when there's nothing else you can bring yourself to eat. I'll do anything for you. But writing it down here it feels like so little. Isn't there anything else? Is there nothing else I can do for you?

It's just after half past three and you're sleeping again, snoring occasionally, I can hear you from the study here, you managed to split your tablet in two, so today you've taken 200 micrograms this morning after breakfast, and I think another 200 now, because your sleep sounds so good, deep and full of rest.

December 2 at 8:40, I land in Guadalajara, it's Monday morning and I've got four nights at a hotel before flying back again on Friday, arriving home in Milan Saturday the 7th in the afternoon. I'm held back for a few minutes in immigration, I've mixed up the flight numbers on the form and need to fill in a new one, but eventually I emerge into the arrivals hall, and in the information I've printed out from the organizers it says I'll be met at the airport by a host who'll be available to me throughout the four days I'm going to be there. But I don't see anyone. A few of those waiting are holding up printed names in front of them, but I can't see mine anywhere. For a moment, I think no one's come, and wonder what to do next, only then I see my name in ballpoint on the outside of a beige-colored folder, held up by a man standing at the back, and the man sees me and I smile and raise my arm in a wave, and he smiles back.

That's when it starts, at the very beginning. The second I look into the eyes of the man with the beige-colored folder and step towards him, that's when it starts. What starts? I don't know. But it wouldn't be accurate to say that something opens up, because it's already opened, even then, at the very beginning. What would that be, that's already opened up? I don't know! Something deep inside him, and inside me. But that's not what I think then, as I step towards him, because I belong to you and this is my last trip before I come home to be with you again, I'm not prepared for anything opening up like that. It happens so quickly. A few steps forward. And yet so slowly. It almost hurts. His eyes, the look in his eyes, rich and vulnerable, there's such a presence about him, I feel it straight away, in my body, it pounds into my loins.

Everyone smiles in Mexico. It feels like I've landed in a place of strong, human warmth. In contrast to Milan, where every day when I go out, when I go down the stairs, I prepare myself for the lack of friendliness there. Milan doesn't do friendly. It's not at all the way Italy-loving Norwegians think, that tired idea of *la dolce vita* all day long. It's just not like that. It's hard living in Milan, really hard, and I've no idea why it has to be like that, I still don't understand it, how being so clammed up and unapproachable apparently can give them such a feeling of satisfaction in life. Because to them it's cultivated, a sign of dignity, not to show their emotions. They're like that at the hospital too, the doctors never smile, the nurses are the same, the cleaners too, and the ones who come and measure your blood pressure, only the guy who comes with the food trolley smiles on occasion, though he's not even Italian, he's from Egypt. But in Mexico people smile, it's like being back in Finnmark, if I smile there, people smile back, and even after I'd only just landed and was waiting for my connection in Mexico City, people smiled at me as I sat in the departure lounge with my suitcase and my turquoise travel pillow around my neck, doubtless looking the worse for wear, they smiled at me then, with no other reason than to smile.

My host is A. He takes my suitcase and I follow him out to the car, we get in and he drives us to where the book fair is, and the hotel. And just getting in the car beside him, we sit there talking as we drive, and it's as if I have to reel in every word I utter from somewhere very far away, as if my thoughts are in the air somewhere, and it doesn't feel like I manage to say anything at all, and his English is full of the sounds of his other language, and just sitting there beside him is so electric. High tension. Energy.

Where does it come from? What is it?

My room isn't ready yet, it's still too early. A suggests we go over to the book fair, it's right next door, so I can start to get my bearings and say hello to people. I don't want to be a burden, I'm used to looking after myself in such places, but he insists, he's my host and it's his job to look after me, and there's this energy between us, and so we go over to the fair and find the stand of my Mexican publishers, and everyone smiles there too, people I've emailed with but never met, they give me hugs, and A is by my side the whole time, or waiting in the background, he gives me such a good feeling, and the writer's lounge has been done out with green palm trees and a little bar, everyone's smiling, and they offer us coffee and tequila, fruit and cookies, but A and I both make do with water and I get my picture taken on a pink sofa against a blue wall, while A sits watching from a sofa opposite, he's a host here at the book fair because he teaches at the university and knows English, the entire book fair is organized by the university, he tells me, and I didn't know, but he's not an academic, he's a businessman and only teaches twice a week, classes in logistics and management.

What would you like to do now? A asks afterwards, still hours before the room will be ready, and I say, I'm sure you've got things to do, I'll be all right, and he says the only thing he needs to do is take a phone call at twelve, a business call, apart from that he's got any amount of time, my job now is to be here with you, he says.

We walk beside each other along the road from the hotel towards the Plaza del Sol, as A tells me it's called, I've said I'd like him to show me a Mexican restaurant within easy walking distance of the hotel, the hotel being right next to the book fair, which is taking place quite a ways from the center of town, and it's hot now, there's a rumble of traffic on the road, palm trees and dust, indigenous people hawking woven armbands and earrings in bright colors on the potholed sidewalk, and there are his trouser legs, he's wearing a navy blue suit and soft black shoes, his left foot, the toe of his shoe, kicking slightly inwards as he walks, which makes me feel a certain tendnerness for him, but I know, because I looked at myself in the mirror when I went to the loo at the book fair so as at last to brush my teeth, while he waited for me outside, that my mascara has run and one eyebrow is smudged, and my makeup's in my suitcase, which is back at the hotel, so I tell myself it doesn't matter, I'm me, whatever state I'm in, and I don't need to be made up for A, because I've got my husband at home in Milan.

It's past five o'clock now, closing in on Sunday evening, the evening before you go into the hospital, it's almost dark outside, and you've woken up, I can hear you in the bathroom, and I get to my feet and open the door of the study and go out into the corridor just as you step out holding your pajama bottoms up with one hand, your clothes far too big for you now, the scar that runs down from your chest, your thin arms, the skin that droops from them now, my love, you say to me, *amore*, as you always write, and I hear the warmth in your voice, I follow you into the bedroom, you get dressed, and I watch as you button up your plaid shirt, you're going to meet your son and his girl-friend at one of the cafés where they make a really good hot chocolate, because you've tried just about everywhere now, and you ask if I want to come with you, but I say I'd rather stay in with a cup of tea and carry on writing, and I can tell from your eyes that you're proud of me, you kiss the tip of my nose and tell me you like my sweater, you enthuse about it, you tell me how elegant it is, that I look like a Nordic intellectual, in such a blue, high-necked sweater. I follow you out into the hall and you put on your woollen suit jacket, your North Face coat on top of that, and then you put on your hat, you have even less hair now, I'm pleased with the way I'm managing my pills, you say, the four hundred microgram ones you've had since yesterday, you tell me you've still got one left, and I thought you'd taken them all, I say, and stroke a finger across your cheek, your eyes peer at me from behind your glasses, you're in such a good mood, so thin and buoyant, and you go out through the door and press the button for the lift, and I wait with you until it comes, and when you step inside, before the door closes, we say the same words to each other, ti amo.

The Plaza del Sol was Guadalajara's first shopping center when it opened, now it's fifty years old, A tells me, and we are too, both fifty years old, and as we walk he tells me he's read *Amor*, as my novel *Love* is titled in Spanish, it's the book I'm here to lauch, at first he read it in English, but he felt there were too many things he hadn't fully understood, and so he read it again in Spanish. He tells me he feels an affinity with Jon, the boy in that novel, because his own mother left him when he was nine years old too. The story and the outer landscape in

which it takes place are very different, he says, but the coldness
of the inner landscape is something he recognizes. In the days
that follow, I use that same observation in all my interviews,
distinguishing between the outer landscape and the inner. Not
because I don't know what to say on my own, but because saying it is to include A in what I say, without anyone else knowing, and without me knowing either, because it's something
I'm not aware of until now, as I sit here writing again in Milan,
this Sunday in January, that from the very first time I saw A, I
wanted only to be near him, to be where he was.

And that's what I managed to write before you got back, I
hear the key in the door and your voice call out, Ciao amore,
it's almost half past six, I look up from the computer and out
through the window, it's completely dark out there, but I can
see the dome of San Lorenzo and the spire of the Duomo, both
are lit up. You come in, because I've left the study door open,
and you've brought a little panetonne home with you, a present
from the parents of your son's girlfriend, And now something
for the writer, you say, and hand me a small oblong box that
looks like it's from a jeweler's, but it's from the coffee shop we

visited a few days ago, that's where you've all been, they make French macaroons there and now you've bought some for me, because when we were there together there were some things we'd have liked to try, only they were sold out, and I stand up with my present and the panettone in my hands and lead you out of the study, because I want to get you away from the computer, I don't want you to see what's on the screen, I haven't told you about A. I open the box in the kitchen, and you've taken a leaflet too, showing the different varieties, and we look at it to find out which is which, but neither of us is ready to taste them yet, so I put them away in the fridge. You say you're going to take the last of your tablets, and I say I'm going to write a bit more. Do you think a kiss will help, you say, with the writing? Of course, I say, and we kiss each other on the mouth and I hug you, drawing you close to me, holding you tight, your entire rickety frame, until I let go, and you go into the bedroom and I come back in here and close the door.

The Plaza del Sol was a conglomeration of shops and cafés and between them an outdoor area with benches to sit on and a small fountain, the sun plaza itself, so I supposed. I looked around and could see a French bakery and a restaurant serving spaghetti and pizza. A had to stop someone and ask, and we then wandered around a bit in search of what turned out to be a place with small lattice windows and heavy timberwork, and I could see waiters inside, dressed in what appeared to be folk costume, white tablecloths on the tables, and heavy, dark-stained chairs. Here we are, said A, you'll get proper Mexican food here. It would soon be time for his phone call, he was going to go inside and take care of it over a cup of coffee, and I told him in the meantime I'd go back and look around the big supermarket we'd gone past just inside the entrance, Give me half an hour, he said, and then he went in. I thought about you, about it being evening in Milan. I thought about how handsome A was, the complicated look in his eyes, but most of all his strong, defining presence, his body next to mine, his thigh under the fabric of his trousers. I thought about how the skin under my chin has begun to droop, but that my face looked such a mess after the journey was something I didn't really see until afterwards when I finally checked into my room, and when I think of the lattice windows of that restaurant A went into, what I remember most is telling myself, Hello, he's not going to be interested in you, he'd think you were too old, come on, don't be so ridiculous. And besides, I didn't want anyone to be interested in me. I didn't want to get involved with any other man. But I couldn't get my head around the electricity. There was such an electricity between us. It was so bewildering, I didn't know what it was I was feeling, only that it was very strong and felt like joy, an unmitigated YES. And I thought about you and went back to the supermarket and found out where the wine was, and they had a Rueda from Spain I decided to buy to keep me company in the hotel room in the evenings, it even had a screw top, only not then, I'd have to come back later, and I looked at the packets of muesli and thought about our breakfasts together during that period when we used to want muesli and berries, and I wondered what had changed, because I always used to want to bring so many things home for you whenever I was away, so that you could see them too, so we could share them for a while and be together in that. But that urge was absent as I passed along the aisles of the supermarket there in the Plaza del Sol on Monday, December 2, in Guadalajara, I felt no urge for it at all, and had no idea why, the only thing I felt, or understood, was that it had nothing to do with A, but with you and me.

Monday, January 13, 9:37, and we're in room number three on the seventeenth floor of the Instituto Nazionale dei Tumori on the Via Giacomo Venezian, you're in bed and have just placed three hundred micrograms under your tongue, but now they come and get you, they want you for something preparatory before the MRI scan later on, they heave you out of bed and the high you've just begun to float away on, we were up at seven, in the taxi by eight, and though you slept a bit last night you're in pain and scared, it would have been so good for you to sleep a bit here, but instead you must find the slippers I put in an Illums Bolighus carrier bag before packing them into your suitcase, and you put on the long dressing gown we've brought with us too, Ti amo, you say, a dopo. And then you're gone and I sit on my own in the room, with the hum of the ventilation system, my laptop on the table in front of me next to a folded white tablecloth, for they come and set the table before meals, spread out the tablecloth, and hand you a white linen napkin, and there's a bowl of fruit too, it was there for us when we came, and next to it the anal tampon you've used for the tests which no one's come to collect yet, and there's your hat, too, and my things, in two tote bags, one from the book fair in Jaipur, a year ago now, the other from the literature festival in Pordenone, *Vent'anni tra le righe*, it says, yellow lettering on black fabric. And then you're back already, you come in and kiss me on the cheek on your way back to bed, and you glance at the laptop, the briefest glance, I don't want you to see the title of the document, but then you're under the covers again with your eyes closed, so tired you are, and I check my phone, there's a message from a friend of ours I texted earlier to say we were here, and now he's replied, *Sei una donna meravigliosa*, he writes, *il tuo amore è così intenso, concentrato. È bene, per lui, avere te*. And I think about A, who I haven't mentioned to anyone, and I look at you lying there in bed, and at last you've fallen asleep, on your side, curled up like a child with one hand under the pillow, under your cheek. I look at you and tears run down my face, yet I feel nothing, no grief, no sadness, I can't feel at all. Is it true, is it actually true, is my love really intense and concentrated?

Returning to the restaurant, I peer through the windows and can't see A anywhere. I go inside, suddenly and keenly fearful, have I kept him waiting too long, has he gone? But then I catch sight of him at a table further inside, white tablecloth, he waves to me and smiles, and I walk up to him, only I realize then he's still on the phone, he's got those wireless earbuds in his ears, and I signal to him that I'll wait for him outside. I stand in the shade up against the wall, outside the door, because I noticed the restaurant had wi-fi, I can connect up there, and I send you a text with a photo from where I'm standing, it's almost eight pm where you are and I know you're going out for something to eat with a friend, you've drawn up a schedule for yourself for each of the six evenings I'm away, yesterday when I was still on the plane you were at a sports pub with your son, you were going to eat burgers and watch a football match, but tonight you're going out with a friend who loves to fine dine just as much as you do, you'll be on your way now, to that new place that's opened on the Corso Colombo, and it makes me happy to think how excited you'll be, that you're going out to do something that brings you pleasure, and you text me back and say that if it's as good as you're hoping, we can go there together one night. Then A appears, all smiles, he's finished his call, Everything okay? I ask, and he tells me he's been speaking with a new worker, a young American woman they've taken on in the property firm he runs on the coast, they sell holiday homes that are very popular with American buyers, so now he's taken this young woman on and needs to get her started, and their talk went well, he seems pleased, but now his attention's on us, Where to now? he asks, and I'm so bewildered by the excitement I feel in my body, I'm nearly trembling, it's lunchtime, only I don't want us to have lunch together, it's all too much as it is, everything that's there between us that I can't fathom, but maybe it's only going on inside me, he's so handsome, he must have a whole entourage of gorgeous young Mexican women, students and all kinds, and he says again that he's here to look after me, only it stresses me out not having a plan and not being sure, maybe he just wants to get away and direct his mind to other things, so I say that perhaps my room will be ready now, and so we walk back to the hotel. As we walk, he asks me a few questions about my writing, we talk about ourselves for a bit, though I can't remember what we tell each other, the whole time we're together our talking feels too light in a way, like something that can only float on top of what's really there, the great unbroached, and then we fall silent, as if being silent together is how we say the most, how we're most truthful together in what is actually there between us and whose exact nature as yet remains unknown to us, all we can do is sense it, and we walk silently at each other's side and I know I'm smiling, it makes me happy to see our legs, our shoes, as we walk along the sidewalk, and when we stop and wait at a pedestrian crossing we look at each other and smile, we both smile. My room is ready and while he waits for the car he's left parked in the hotel garage to be driven to the entrance I say I hope he'll be coming to the dinner that evening, the dinner my publishers are putting on, they invited him to come along when we visited their stand at the book fair earlier on, and back home in Milan we talked about that dinner and you kept telling me I should go, that it would be fun, it's something they do every year, you told me, on the first evening of the book fair, and there are always lots of people there, I've been invited together with the Norwegian delegate from NORLA and my Spanish publisher, they'll be there too, Come with us, I tell A, it would make me so happy. And it's true, I can feel it. But am I invited? A asks, and I say, Yes, they asked you earlier on at the stand, remember, of course you're invited, and again I tell him how nice it would be if he came with me, and at last he agrees, though not without hesitation, and when he sees how pleased I am, he agrees more emphatically, and from then on that's what propels me through the remaining hours of the day, the thought of seeing him again and being close to him, that these strong feelings, whose exact nature as yet remains unknown to me, may continue.

It's five to twelve, you're asleep, your body twitches, it never used to, but now your body twitches and I can't hold your hand in the night they way we did before, because now your fingers will suddenly start tapping in my palm and it wakes me up, Don't leave me, I used to say, don't find someone else, and you'd always say to me then, You're so close to me, we're so close there's no room for anyone else between us. When I think of you saying that to me I always see you sitting on the sofa in our old apartment, and I realize it's because that was where we lived before you were ill. We were still living there when we found out you were ill, and you were ill when we moved out, and in our new home, which is where we decided all the colors ourselves, the tiles on the bathroom floor, the kitchen, and the way we wanted the bookshelves, or rather it was me who decided, a few days before your surgery, at the superstore together with the surveyor from the building firm that was doing the place up, you were there too, but you were in such pain that you spent the whole time sitting down, and then you got tired and were cross with yourself, so it was me who decided on our behalf, I've done it before, and it was no time to dither, I went for colors I like, simple design, and wouldn't listen to you when suddenly you pitched in wanting patterns and things I could see weren't going to work, whereas I'd have listened to you before and we'd have found a compromise, but there just wasn't room for that then, we needed to get things lined up, we needed a home, and even then I knew you were probably going to die. When you were on your way home after having been to see your friend who's a doctor, you'd been waiting all summer for her to come home so you could go and see her, the one who at last and straight away knew what was wrong with you, her father having died from cancer of the pancreas and her brother a surgeon who carries out the same kind of interventions as you'd soon be having, after you'd vomited all that blood in early September she finally came back and you went to see her and she immediately sent you for a CT scan and the next day the results came through and her brother happened to be there too even though he lives in Switzerland and you looked at the images together, why wasn't I there with you, and you could all see the tumor and how big it was, but also that there might be a chance with surgery, which isn't always the case, and you phoned me when you were on your way home from there on the Metro and told me you had pancreatic cancer and I googled it before coming to meet you by the Metro stairs and it said so very plainly on the computer screen that this was something only few people survive, I knew this as I was walking towards you, and you'd got there before me, so we met halfway, on the sidewalk, your face seemed like it was swollen in a way, and your coat was hanging open, and you hugged me tight, but we didn't talk about death, not then, and not since, and after we moved into the new apartment I made so many trips to IKEA, taking the train from Romolo, walking by the long, straight road between the warehouses and bushes and fencing, to the boxy blue and yellow building at the end, taking photos I'd send you, because you were at home, asking what you thought, phoning you, and eventually all you could say was you trusted me, you decide, and I bought lamps for all the rooms and lugged them home in those big blue bags, the bigger items were delivered, and in this apartment you've never not been ill, never, the apartment we'd so looked forward to sharing together, in this apartment all you've done is get more and more ill.

You sit up in bed, they've brought some food, but only for me, you've got to fast before the examination, only then the nurse comes and says it'll be another two to three hours yet, so if you want you can have just a bite of something, and you say you fancy a brioche, so I go down to the hospital snack bar by the entrance and buy a pain au chocolat, you wanted one with jam in it, but that's all they've got, and when I come back you sit up in bed and start eating it, while I munch broccoli and zucchini here at the table where I sit and write. And then you say, I'm not actually that hungry, I'm scared. Yes, I say, and look at you, and we say nothing for a moment. What are you scared of, I say then, thinking death, only you say you're scared you'll have to have more surgery, that's what's on your mind, another operation, and I just blurt out then that they won't be doing that, they won't operate twice, because that's what I've read, they might perhaps operate to facilitate the passage of food if there are tumors that get bigger and block the way, or to ease the pressure on nerves and lessen pain, procedures that are meant to alleviate rather than cure, that's what I've read, but all I say is that they won't operate again, and at that moment you look at me as if suddenly there's something you've understood, or seen, But what will they do then, you say, if they won't operate and the chemo doesn't work? *Are they just going to let me die?* you say, looking like this is a competely new thought, as if you've ventured into an area that until now has been cordoned off, where you've never set foot before and have no clue, your face looks like it's collapsing in on itself and there's nothing there for you to hold onto, I'm scared for you then, scared that now you're going to be scared and distraught and helplessly adrift inside, and I'm surprised at myself, haven't I been wanting us to make contact with the reality of this, to look openly into each other's eyes, be together in the way things actually are, and yet here I am, scared by your mere mention of death, your even entertaining the possibility of it, and I feel I must get you away from there at once, because I'm not that resilient, not at all, and when at the next moment you seem to leap inside yourself, across to the opposite place where hope resides, and say you're sure everything will be all right, all I can say is I think so too, even though I don't.

That night, we're allowed to go home after all, you didn't have to sleep over at the hospital, the plan now is that all the doctors with responsibility for you are going to meet and con-fer on how best to move forward, the MRI revealed what the increased pain you've been having and the new lump on the right-hand side of your abdomen have suggested, that the effects of the chemo are diminishing, the cancerous tissue has spread and the lump is a new tumor inside the big stomach muscle, there's no CA 19-9 level noted in your discharge summary, they simply haven't measured it, there was no point, the MRI told them what they needed to know, under Treatment it says they'll now consider experimental therapy, I'm not sure what that means, maybe that the normal treatment isn't working anymore and they want to try something different and see what happens, and that night is no night for you, it holds neither sleep nor rest, a sense of panic has gripped you, now and then I'm awake with you, you talk to me and I try to answer without frightening you, Am I going to die, you ask, and I tell you that's what they've been saying ever since they discovered how it had spread after the surgery, that you won't recover from this, but it's as if somehow you haven't thought about that as death until now, you've been thinking it was all such a long way off, a lifetime, You're going to die too, you say to me, Yes, I say, and that's all I say, because where you are now it's impossible to reach you with words, and you seem not to notice me touching you either, holding you, you're in a place where there's no one else but you. At the hospital, they gave you two packets of 200 microgram tablets, normally a packet lasts you twenty-four hours, but before seven o'clock both packets are empty and they haven't helped, you say, it hurts so much, and just before eight-thirty you phone the oncologist, the one with the curly hair and brown eyes, he came in to see me after they took you away for the MRI, it was after you got scared and I got scared by your being scared. He told me they were going to stick to the same course, keeping you reassured, and asked if I was in agreement with that and I said I was, and now you phone him, I can hear you talking to him as I stand in the living room, and what am I doing to you, I ask myself, what right have I to decide what information comes through to you about your own life, and I go from the living room into the hall to listen in as you talk to him, you're in the bedroom, spaced out on the medication, and sound quite composed, you say you're phoning because you didn't get the chance to speak yesterday and are wondering how things stand, and he explains something to you and you listen, and eventually you thank him and wish him a pleasant day, and when you hang up you come into the living room feeling relieved, he wasn't alarmed, you say, there's been a setback, but not that serious, you seem pleased, and I ask myself why you didn't probe more directly as to the outlook, how much time he thinks you've got. If you'd asked him straight out he'd have been compelled then to give you a straight answer, and that's what he said too, the oncologist, when he came to see me there in our room at the hospital when you weren't there, He's not asking many questions, the doctor said, and neither are you, not even now. I feel complicit in this and unsure if I'm doing the right thing, what is the right thing even, maybe there isn't just one thing that's the right thing, I've always thought there was until now, that the right thing is always to look the truth in the eye and live with it the way it is, regardless of how much it hurts, but even if I still think that's right, maybe it's not for me to decide what's right for you. You're the most intelligent man I know, and if you're not asking it must be because something in you chooses not to know more.

Do you believe in synchronicity? A asked as we sat in the car on our way from the airport, and I said yes, I did, and after that we talked no more about it, and in fact I can't really remember that much of what we said a lot of the time we were together, what was important, what still is important with A, isn't on the level of talk, it has to do with presence, energy, and I believe in that.

When I met you four years ago it was all to do with presence then too, all I knew was that I wanted to be with you, meeting you was like gazing into gentle hills in a Welsh landscape, and I wanted to go there, to live there, and it wasn't something I thought, but something I felt, I knew it in my body, though I was quite unable to put it into words for myself, it was simply the case. That I yearned to belong, to be inseparable from someone, I knew that, I'd felt it for some time, but it wasn't until I wrote *Novel. Milan* that I began to understand more, and I could only get close to these places in me because you allowed me to get close to you.

It was when I was writing *Over the Mountain* that I met you. I wrote myself into a place then where our coming together became possible, I knew that the work I was doing in writing that novel, approaching the girl-child parts of me from which I've detached myself all my life, despised and shunned, was in order to ready myself to live in nearness to another person and love them. Because if I couldn't be near the vulnerable, soft and silly girly parts of me, the parts that so yearned for affection, how could I believe I could ever allow another person to be? Another person can't make me love what I despise about myself, therefore if I hate myself I can never feel loved. And I longed for someone to love. And when the novel was nearly finished I met you, and meeting you was to live out what the novel was a movement towards, which was belonging. And while we live our lives in days, the life I live in the novel, as I'm writing it, is perhaps the deepest, most truthful and most precise expression of the life that goes on in those days, before, during, and after the novel. The novel is the life I live on the inside and it fetches things up from different times and separate layers that I often don't realize need to meet, so that I can be with them, the way you might sit on the edge of a bed in the evening and hold the hand of a child, just being there, for the novel possesses an insight so much deeper than my own, and because it's in touch with this very life force itself, it knows so much better than I do where the wave of each new novel is going to take me. But since I finished writing *Novel. Milan*, which was when you became ill, it's been completely impossible for me to write. I braced myself and then you came, and your coming meant that I moved forward, I came home. But now you're going to die, you, who allowed me at last to find that home with you, and how am I going to move forward from that, here and now?

Silence! Stop sign – zone border! Birgitta Trotzig wrote. I haven't had the energy to keep up my notebook either. In what little I've managed to put down there, under November 29, it says:

It's as if the writing in me has withdrawn – tactfully, almost – not wanting to bother me in these times.

November 29 was a Friday, and three days later, Monday, December 2, I meet A. What my notebook tells me is that I'm not in touch with my life force. And that's the force that's awakened in me by meeting A, it's meeting A that propels me into writing this, it begins like a fire between my legs and radiates upwards through my abdomen, making me laugh again, making me feel happy.

We saw each other only four times in all. The first time was at the airport and the few short hours we spent together before I could check into the hotel, the second time was the dinner that same evening, and the third time was when he showed me the old town in Guadalajara. I'd been doing interviews at the book fair all morning and into the afternoon, but at four o'clock when I was finished he picked me up at the hotel and off we went in his car, he parked in an underground parking lot from where we emerged directly into the historic center, a large area in the middle of the city where motor vehicles are prohibited, and we strolled around there, drawn on by a particularly colorful building we wanted to look at, or a street we wanted to go down because of the little crooked trees that grew there, and we lingered at the fruit stalls of the indigenous women, and if they had something I'd never seen or tasted before, A would buy some in a bag for me to try, and we went inside a food hall crammed with nacho bars that were full of smoke from the wood burners, and people perched on stools, eating from tin plates, the counters displayed meat and offal, we saw intestines and I had no idea they were twisted like braided hair, there were brains and tongues too, and the people behind the counters stood and smiled at us and said things in Spanish which A translated when I didn't understand, and eventually we didn't know what else to do, so we sat down on a bench, sat there for an hour perhaps, while the sun went down, and I tried to take some photos, because the light was soft and low, but they came out nothing like it looked, there were some children playing, and a fountain where couples kept coming and having their picture taken, and we watched them and looked sideways at each other, then looked out across the square again, we just sat there quite still, without talking, and I felt such a happiness, I don't think I've ever known anything like it, it was as if everything was love, in that hour, as if the whole world was nothing but love, hallowed was how it felt, so immense, and tears ran down my cheeks, because in that hour I existed only there, and was *immersed in love*.

A knows I'm married, I've told him about you, how we met, and that I now live here in Milan with you, I've told him you're very ill and that you were supposed to have come with me, only it wasn't possible. The last time I'm with A is Wednesday evening, he's going away on a trip early Thursday morning, it's been planned for quite a while, and I've been allocated a new guide from the university, but we want to meet and say good-bye, that's why he comes. I've been up since five that morning, unable to sleep from the jet lag, have run for an hour on the treadmill and showered and talked to you on the phone, before I go for breakfast it's close to midnight where you are, nearly a night less to wait now, you say, and I say I love you, and you say I love you more than anything else, and then you lie down to sleep at home in our bed and at half past eight I'm picked up by the teacher from a school I'm going to visit as part of my book fair program, there's so much traffic, so many traffic jams in Guadalajara, but slowly we make our way out of the city, it's a two-hour drive to get there, a tiny road at the end into the mountains, then two hours back again. I have more interviews to do in the afternoon, but the last two I've rescheduled to give me an hour with A before going out for dinner with my Spanish publisher, an hour and a half in fact, only there's traffic and A is flustered by the time he finally arrives, more than a quarter of our time has gone already, this feeling I sense we both have that what we do together, that our being together, is so important. I want to be outside and so we go to the shop across the road and buy a beer for me, mineral water for A, who doesn't drink, and peanuts for A too, he bought peanuts the evening before as well, when we were in the center of town, he ate some and then gave the rest to a man who came begging as we sat on the bench, and then we sit down with our beer and mineral water on a wall by the road as the sun goes down, it's rush hour and the traffic moves slowly by us, but at that moment there's only us and I notice I'm touching him, touching his arm as we speak, stroking his back, my arm just reaching out, and we touch each other with our eyes without speaking, and I'm relieved to be going out for dinner with my publisher, because it'll keep me from A and something I'm not sure I'd be able to stop myself from doing, something I really don't want to do. Because I want to be with you. I want to be yours alone and for nothing to come between us ever. I want to be with you always. And it's what I've been doing and have been all this time. I tell A how ill you really are. He's brought his copy of *Amor* with him and I write a dedication on the title page, I write: Inside me we'll always be sitting on this wall next to each other. A gives me a letter. And then darkness has fallen and I look at the time, I'm already a quarter of an hour late for my appointment, we stand up and cross the road back to the hotel, dodging the traffic, and then we're not on our own anymore, my publisher comes out to greet us, she's been waiting for me and A, and I say goodbye to him as she looks on, we kiss each other on the cheek and A gets into his car, pulls away, and is gone. After that I don't see A again. But the fire stays in me, it's alive.

Evening has come in Milan, I've been writing since just before three, now it's almost eight, I see the dome of San Lorenzo all lit up, myself reflected in the pane with my reading glasses on. When I came back from the gym you were asleep, it was just after twelve then, rest at last after that terrible night, and this morning before I went out I gave you an extra morphine patch on your shoulder now that you've run out of pills, and I come to your bedside now and smooth a finger gently over your cheek, you stir, only for your eyes to close again as you look at me, you force them open again, peering out from far within, Now I feel better, you say, you remembered you had some anxiety pills and you suppose they must have worked. An hour later you get up and put on your clothes and shoes to go to the office, and I follow you to the door and wait for the lift with you, Ti amo, we say. And now it's evening and you're home again, you let yourself in just after six and come straight to my desk and kiss me on the neck, Today's been quite good, you say, holding a bag from the pharmacy in your hand, they'd managed to get some packets for you, I'll take a pill now and go for a lie down, you say, and I carry on with my writing. This was almost two hours ago, it's five to eight now, I've been writing this all that time, sometimes hearing you, your breathing, the odd snore before you're quiet again.

Today is Wednesday, January 15, it's two days since we were at the hospital when they did the MRI scan showing your cancer has spread, and I'd thought before Monday that after the scan, after Monday, something would have changed, that we'd have entered a new phase, only now I'm no longer sure, it's like everything just carries on the same as before. This morning you went back to the hospital, you had a ten o'clock appointment with two pain specialists to map out where to go from here. And me, what am I going to do? Where do I go from here?

When I touched down at Malpensa, Saturday, December 7, you were there to meet me. Only coming home wasn't at all how I'd imagined it when I went away. I'd been so looking forward to getting all my traveling done and finally, finally being with you. But there was this new fire in my body and that energy was so different from yours, you, who have so little strength and must rest such a lot and are often so far away in that spacy state the morphine puts you in. Ever since you first got ill I've followed along with you, followed your energy levels, and you've been in such pain with all that was happening to your body, the catastrophe of that, and the long incision they made to remove things from inside you, I wanted to be so near to you, so I had to follow along with you wherever you were, and I did, because it was the only thing I wanted, I who had found you at last and come home. But after Guadalajara I realized that I'd doused my own life fire in order to be in touch with yours. And that suddenly there in Mexico mine flamed up again, while you continued to be ill, in such a low place, and it opened up a distance between us.

I didn't want to drink in the evenings anymore, the way I've been doing ever since you got ill, all I wanted was a glass of wine with dinner, I was focused, I started looking for books to read that could nourish me as I moved towards a new novel, the one I'm imagining which isn't this one, I wanted to inhabit myself again. I'd said to A that I'd be silent, I wanted to be with you, close to you again, and I didn't want to go behind your back with anything, I really didn't want that, although I'm already hiding your death from you, who do I think I am. But I know that being told I'd met another man would be worse for you in a way than becoming aware that you're dying, even though I haven't done anything more than kiss him goodbye on the cheek, because suddenly the closeness we've shared, which has been our we, us, the closest and strongest bond in all the world, suddenly we'd be blasted apart, by my having shared a closeness with another. I'll never tell you that.

A was far away, but I had this fire in me, it was mine and it kept on burning, I felt its warmth between my legs at night and it felt like I was adrift on an endless wave of orgasm, and then one night I had a dream, it was after New Year's, more than a month after I'd met A and left him again. I dreamt that I woke up and checked my phone and there were three messages from A, no text in them, only images, photos. It was such a vivid dream. The first image was of A's hand, the back of his hand, with a big, black spider on it. The next image was similar, A's hand again, though a bit further away, only now there were five spiders, they formed a pattern, and in the background there was water, as if the picture had been taken by the sea. The last image was from under the water, taken as if at that exact moment when a person walking into the sea stumbles and falls and the water is pierced by rays of light and everything is blues and yellows and greens.

The next day I wrote the first words of this, whatever it is.

I love you, I wrote. I love you, I write, I say, when you come through the door in the evenings. You still come through the door when it's evening. For now, you're here, with me. And what I've been writing is the most truthful way I've been able to be with you, with all that cannot be said between us in our days together. I'm not going anywhere, I'm here, and I'll be here all the way until it's you who isn't here anymore.

From my notebook, October 24, on the train back to you from Ravenna:

Bleak, drizzle. 9 am walked to Basilica di San Vitale and Mausoleo di Galla Placidia. The blue blue vaulted ceiling of the mausoleum with its shining stars of gold and a cross at the apex. You've wanted to bring me here and show me this from the very start. And now I'm seeing it on my own.

(Yesterday I saw Dante's grave.)

In the San Vitale – the way the great marble blocks of the pillars possess a quieter beauty than the glittering mosaics. The mottled markings in the marble are just there, silent and displayed, defenseless, and what was hidden within the stone, the veins, the figures they trace, is exposed now for all time, laid bare, halted in once so sweeping, now dissected movements through the stone. And what we see is the cross section, the wound, and the beauty of what simply exists, neither devised nor constructed, merely disclosed. This is. These veins in marble. This traced figure. And you are somewhere between the two. Between the silent pillars of marble and the gleaming mosaics of the chancel. Between everything that is, you come towards me, are with me, are you.

archipelago books

is a not-for-profit literary press devoted to
promoting cross-cultural exchange through innovative
classic and contemporary international literature
www.archipelagobooks.org